M000283411

PRAISE FOR *HALFWAY HOUSE*

'Lou O'Dowd ... is a chaotic, sexually incontinent, drinking, drug-taking liar, yet she is irresistible and very funny ... The set-up is fascinating, the narrative is both fast-moving and convincing, and the events Lou has to face are highly dramatic' *Literary Review*

'Tense, claustrophobic and laugh-out-loud funny. Helen FitzGerald is an amazingly talented writer. I love her work'
Michael Wood

'A genius combination of horror, humour and humanity'
B M Carroll

'Outrageous, hilarious and dark as hell – this is Helen FitzGerald on absolute top form' Doug Johnstone

'Fast, addictive, with brilliantly diverse characters and a rich vein of dark humour, I tore through this book in a single sitting. A long overdue book from a master of satire. Fans of the author are going to love it. Most heartily recommended'
Jen Med's Book Reviews

'It's a thriller, it's a tragedy, it's a dark comedy, it has tons of elements from different genres but they all blend together marvellously, and FitzGerald's dark and acerbic humour is a juicy blood-red cherry on top of this fabulous cake. Recommended, in particular for jaded readers who want to shake things up'
From Belgium with Booklove

PRAISE FOR HELEN FITZGERALD

'The main character is one of the most extraordinary you'll meet between the pages of a book' Ian Rankin

'Sharp, shocking and savagely funny. Helen FitzGerald is a wonderfully original storyteller' Chris Whitaker

'A new novel from Helen FitzGerald is *always* a major event. *Keep Her Sweet* is magnificent' Mark Billingham

'I devoured *Keep Her Sweet* … shite parenting and a dysfunctional sister relationship goes to fatal extremes' Erin Kelly

'At turns wickedly funny, breath-stealingly tense and utterly chilling … a book you'll want to talk about' Miranda Dickinson

'Dark humour sings from the pages … balanced by unexpected moments of levity that often give you empathy for even the most unpleasant of her characters' Russel McLean

'Not for the faint-hearted, but definitely for those who love deadly, dysfunctional families, whip-smart writing, and their stories dark, dark, deliciously dark' Amanda Jennings

'A crazy but addictive, dark and funny read!' Louise Beech

'I'm a huge fan of Helen FitzGerald's offbeat characters and mordant wit … the author at her masterly best' Louise Candlish

'Dark, atmospheric and terrifying' Ambrose Parry

'A dark, comic masterpiece that manages to be both excruciatingly tense and laugh-out-loud funny' Mark Edwards

'Simply stunning. Dark, uncompromising, funny … Mary is one my favourite characters of recent times. Always real, always honest, always superb' Luca Veste

'Took me on such a journey and a range of emotions!! Laughing, cringing and hesitant all at the same time … Totally gripping' Madeleine Black

'Exhilarating!' S. E. Lynes

'Helen FitzGerald has an uncanny ability to balance savagery and hilarity … an absolute banger of a book' Matt Wesolowski

'Very dark, very funny and very original. Helen FitzGerald is one of a kind, and a welcome breath of fresh air' S. J. I. Holliday

'Toughminded and funny, but laced with serious intent' *Daily Mail*

'Helen FitzGerald's novels are wonderful. You never know what she is going to come out with next' *The Times* Crime Club

'Compelling' *Independent*

'This frenetic novel's strongest assets are its sheer verbal energy and the acerbic views of its heroine, who resembles a female Frankie Boyle' *Sunday Times*

'A scandalously rude comic masterpiece' *Daily Telegraph*

'Sublime … a foul-mouthed, satirical revenge thriller' *Guardian*

'Tantalisingly powerful' *The Times*

'It's dark, yes, but with an effusive sense of humanity at its heart that makes this read highly recommended' *Mystery People*

'Domestic life is rarely served up quite so dark as this – but that only makes you hungry for more' *Sun*

'From the author of *The Cry*, and laced with pitch-dark acerbic humour, the classic thriller gets a hell of a twist' *Heat*

'The plotting is intricate and beautifully handled, and the narrative pace is absolutely breakneck … a wonderful, energetic, hard-hitting and deeply funny novel' *The Big Issue*

'Intensely dramatic and yet oh-so convincing … *Keep her Sweet* is fabulously entertaining, and yet as confrontational and powerful as heck' LoveReading

HALFWAY HOUSE

ABOUT THE AUTHOR

Helen FitzGerald is the bestselling author of thirteen adult and young-adult thrillers, including *The Donor* (2011) and *The Cry* (2013), which was longlisted for the Theakstons Old Peculier Crime Novel of the Year and adapted for a major BBC drama. Her 2019 dark-comedy thriller *Worst Case Scenario* was a Book of the Year in the *Literary Review*, *Herald Scotland, Guardian* and *Daily Telegraph*, shortlisted for the Theakston's Old Peculier Crime Novel of the Year, and won the CrimeFest Last Laugh Award. The critically acclaimed *Ash Mountain* (2020) and *Keep Her Sweet* (2022) soon followed.

Helen worked as a criminal-justice social worker for over fifteen years. She grew up in Victoria, Australia, and now lives in Glasgow with her husband. Follow Helen on Twitter @FitzHelen and at facebook.com/fitzgerald.helen.

Also by Helen FitzGerald and available from Orenda Books

Worst Case Scenario

Ash Mountain

Keep Her Sweet

HALFWAY HOUSE

HELEN FITZGERALD

ORENDA
BOOKS

Orenda Books
16 Carson Road
West Dulwich
London SE21 8HU
www.orendabooks.co.uk

First published in the United Kingdom by Orenda Books, 2024

A catalogue record for this book is available from the British Library.

ISBN 978-1-914585-70-8
eISBN 978-1-914585-71-5

Typeset in Garamond by www.typesetter.org.uk

Printed and bound by CPI Group (UK) Ltd, Croydon CR0 4YY

For sales and distribution, please contact info@orendabooks.co.uk

For my beautiful mum, Isabel Ann FitzGerald,
who gave me a love of language and the confidence
to play with it. Miss you, Mum.

PROLOGUE

She wasn't coming over well.

'Some people have described you as a *psychopath*,' the interviewer said.

This woman had been so friendly before the cameras came on ('How was Tuscany, tell me everything?') Now, she was a mean girl with an iPad: 'Hashtag SugarBabyKiller,' she said. 'Hashtag Impaler.'

Lou remembered her father's most recent advice: 'Only answer direct questions.' She said nothing but feared her anger was showing. She must not sit so stiffly. She must try to look victim-esque, by being nice, on the inside. She must listen to the mean girl, and then say something to prove she'd listened.

She couldn't think of a thing to say, probably because she had failed to listen. She would listen now.

But what was the point, trying to be likeable, looking the way she did? She'd bought a new suit for this interview – grey, understated, serious, not attractive or murderous in the least. She'd straightened her hair and pulled it behind her ears. She'd used concealer under her eyes, nothing more. Then someone grabbed her in the green room and dragged her to hair and makeup. She should have stopped them but there were mirrors and lights and bottles and brushes. It was irresistible; a trap.

'Just for the cameras,' they'd said, glossing and curling her hair, piling on eyebrows and lashes and lips – and, ta-da, she was Lou the Impaler, Hashtag LusciousLou, Hashtag YesPleaseLouise. Hashtag…

'A master manipulator, a cold-blooded killer,' the mean girl said.

There was a dead man in her head now, skewered. She needed to firm up her face, which should be sad, and sorry. She needed to focus, for *Sixty Minutes*. She must loosen her neck and shoulders and she must listen to the mean girl.

She'd asked her a question – at last – but Lou hadn't heard it. It was probably something about the murder: *Where did she learn how to do that?!* Or it might have been about being cast out into the sugar-baby badlands. People loved hearing about all that. Or maybe the mean girl had just asked about Edinburgh, where it all began, or at least where it all began again. That sinister word: Edinburgh. She focused – and the interviewer repeated it. Edinburgh: the most beautiful city in the world, the city she had chosen as hers.

CHAPTER ONE

Two Months Earlier

Lou was going to remember people's birthdays. She was going to fall in love enough to share a bed. There'd be no need to cry or to lie for the new Lou, skipping across the grass in The Meadows, taking in a show, posing at the castle, as she no doubt would do. She imagined herself each night before falling asleep: linking hands with two great friends at Hogmanay, part of a huge circle of beaming Scots – *May auld acquaintance be forgot* – moving in and out, the circle as one, voices as one, in and out, faster, faster, auld. lang. syne. One time – honestly, it happened twice – she had a tartan orgasm.

She was already transforming into her new self. The old Lou would never have gone for a job like the one she was about to interview for. With two minutes to go, Lou closed the blinds to shut out the every-city night-lights of Melbourne. She styled a slapdash ponytail, took a seat, and opened the link. She was the first on screen, so she froze, maintained her pose. She must not loosen the thong sawing away at her crack, she must not scratch the pubes that were growing back. In the last two weeks she'd applied for every lowly admin and retail job in and around Edinburgh. No luck so far – seventeen rejections, twenty-four ghostings. Catering and hospitality were out – she'd had enough of smiling at rich people. In despair, she had widened the search to include the care sector, and: bingo! An interview. It sounded exciting, it was in the centre of the most beautiful city in the world, and it was only three night shifts a week. Four days adventuring, every single week. Farewell unhappy idiot Lou and all the people she knew. She would get this job. And she would never – ow, god, she wriggled – *ever*, wear a thong again.

A skinny, spiky redhead – Polly, seventy-ish – appeared on screen, sipping her coffee. 'Hello,' she said, no smile. 'Just waiting on David, won't be long.'

It was morning on the other side of the world, in that fairy-tale land as far away as you could get. Imagine, she'd be jetlagged soon. 'I'm so jetlagged,' she would say as she sipped a pint of ale with an unforgettable friend in an ancient pub.

Polly coughed. She must be a smoker, nearer fifty than seventy.

Lou could hear a man's voice in the background:

'Morning!' the man said.

Polly's face got nicer as she turned her head. 'Hey, pal, just doing interviews,' she said.

'Oops, so sorry,' said the voice off screen. 'I'll pop the kettle on, and I'm closing the door behind me.'

'Cheers, pal,' said Polly, her face pinched once more. She was reading something that disgusted her then looking up at Lou without changing her face. There was an old calendar on the flaky wall behind her. 2019.

'Hello.' David had a Mallen streak, a lopsided head, cool jacket, no tie. There were bookshelves in his background – *Social Work Practice in the Criminal Justice System, Scottish Criminal Law Essentials*; *Race, Gender and—*

She had read enough.

'You must be Lou. How are you doing?'

'Good, thanks.' She must find cleverer things to say.

'Nice to meet you,' he said. 'I'm David Wallace, general manager and this is Polly Grange, project manager of SASOL.'

This stood for Supported Accommodation Services for Offenders, Lothian. Lou did not expect it to be pronounced 'sarsehole'. She bit her lip.

'As you'll know from the job description, SASOL is a five-bed unit for very-high-risk offenders.'

She hadn't noticed the word 'very' in the advertisement. By accident, she might be about to get an important job, a meaningful job, an exciting job – not with bad boys, but with 'very' bad boys. She had tingles.

'It's not like other services,' David said. 'There are only three in the country: us; our women's unit nearby; and another non-profit up north. This job is at the men's unit, doing three night shifts a week. The residents in the unit have served more than four years in prison and have been released on licence with a condition of residence for twelve months. Most are MAPPA level two or three.'

She would have to look that up.

'And all have stringent licence conditions such as MFMC and DASS…'

And that and that.

'…a 10pm to 7am curfew, as well as various additional restrictions regarding internet use, employment, leisure activities, contact with family members, etcetera. The role of the night-care worker is to ensure that SASOL is a safe place for all residents, to offer support and advice in relation to any risks and needs, to promote rehabilitation, to keep records, do handover meetings with day staff and to respond to any incidents. How this goes is I'm going to ask you three questions, then Polly is going to ask you three questions. It should take fifteen minutes. My first question relates to values.'

This all felt very giggly; took her back to parent-teacher meetings – Lou against all the adults, all the adults against Lou; every teacher wondering the same thing: *How can Lou be so unhappy and disruptive when her mother is so dedicated and loving, and when her father is hilarious and a spunk?*

'Your reference from the café was very good,' David said. 'No problems there. But the second reference has raised some concerns.'

Oh dear.

'"To whom it may concern."' David put on his glasses and cleared his throat. '"We are managing partners of Genova's Limited, a property group that manages apartment complexes and budget hotels, all of which are located in the Melbourne metropolitan area. We are writing to confirm that Miss Louise O'Dowd worked for the company for two years. Her position was project worker at North Melbourne House, a hundred-bed homeless hostel. Her main duty was to deep-clean rooms that had been soiled by overdoses, violent incidents and suicide attempts. She also dealt with the challenging behaviour of very-high-risk criminals. Miss O'Dowd proved herself to be strong of stomach and we have no hesitation recommending her for demeaning care tasks in a dangerous setting.

'"Frieda and Alan Bainbridge."'

Alan Bainbridge was Lou's boyfriend – till she found out he was married. Then he was her sugar daddy – till his wife found out. Lou had accepted that it was over and that there would be no contact. She was excellent at closure – a little too good some might say. She certainly wasn't stalkerish. All she did was send one teensy text. She was moving to the UK. She wanted to do office work. She needed to fill in the two-year gap in her CV. He employed hundreds of people. Could he please give her a reference?

One hour later, the above appeared in Lou's Gmail – not from Alan, but from his wife, the formidable Frieda.

David, SASOL's general manager, took off his glasses and had a sip of water. 'Is this for real, or does your old employer have difficulty with English?'

'Polish is Frieda's first language. She must have written it.'

'Why did she describe working with the homeless as demeaning? How do you feel about this kind of work?'

Lou had an answer for this. 'The Bainbridges are money-makers,' she said, 'that's all they see. They're rich because money matters to them more than compassion. My values are very different. Working with the homeless, as with ex-offenders, is a privilege.'

David and Polly clearly liked what she was saying. She could relax, let the rest of the interview flow.

Conflict resolution?

Easy. She thought about how she felt at the last meal she had with her parents, how she lowered her voice till her dad did too and how she breathed in and out for a while instead of stabbing her mother with a fork.

Building relationships?

A cinch. Lou was an army brat, made friends more quickly than cups of tea. (She didn't add that she was even better at discarding them.)

How about ethical dilemmas?

Bring 'em on. Lou's only work experience, apart from the café, was as a sugar baby. She was one big walking, fucking ethical dilemma. Who was she to judge bad boys when she was a bad girl? She didn't tell them any of this, of course, but she did say all the right things.

Or she thought she did. She might have said all the wrong things. She tossed and turned till 7am, when a message pinged in from Polly: *Congratulations. We were very impressed by your work experience and your enthusiasm.*

Lou pounced from the bed. She had a proper job. In a faraway land. 'Alexa, play The Proclaimers'. She danced for an hour. She was on her way from misery to happiness. She was the sparkly new employable Lou.

Fuck you, Frieda.

She had no idea what she wanted to be when she grew up, but maybe this was it. Not this job, necessarily, but in the same field. This was her way into criminal justice. Criminal. Justice. She would stop people doing bad things. She would help people find good things about themselves. She would find herself, grow up. Nah, delete that one. She was going on an adventure. She did not have to grow up. She was only twenty-three, for fuck's sake.

Lou spent the following week throwing things out, giving things away, cleaning, and ironing labels (*LOU O'DOWD*) onto every single item of her clothing, even her pants, a habit her father encouraged before a move. When she had finally finished packing, she popped her last bottle of Alan-bought champagne and danced around her bright-white and empty love nest. Goodbye Alan, goodbye Frieda, Jane from swimming, Billy the bike-maintenance guy. *Lou was here 2023*, she scratched under the breakfast bar. She then checked that all the rooms were clean and empty, that she had her passport, her ticket, phone, chargers, cabin bag, suitcase, etcetera. She stood on the balcony one last time, bubbly in hand, the city skyline behind her, and posted a selfie on Instagram:

Here's looking up your kilt, I'm off to Edinburgh,

Lou.

CHAPTER TWO

Lou could do with a barley sugar. Must be all the excitement. Nothing to do with entering international arrivals alone, finding the check-in gate alone, walking towards the mile-long queue, alone.

She scoured the huge hall for her mum, who was always there to see her off, no matter where she was going. She looked for her dad, usually holding the makings of a picnic. No sign. Her parents had not come to surprise her. She had lost them too. No wonder, after that terrible dinner in Port Melbourne. Two years ago, it was.

They had arrived in Melbourne frazzled, which was no surprise – it was her mother's job to navigate, even though she never showed any interest in where she was supposed to be going next. She was a 'present' person. A little bit away with the fairies. Not someone who should be given the task of chief navigational officer, especially when they didn't have satnav in the car.

'There are no signals on a battlefield,' her father always said.

Lou wasn't sure this sounded true. Also, her father had never been on a battlefield. What was true was that both parents disliked the internet. They preferred music, dancing, an hour a week of live television, gardening, going for long hikes, the smell of a good hardback, home-made sourdough, the feel of a Melways map and bucketloads of stress.

Lou's mum always took on the navigation task as best and as calmly as she could, unfolding unwieldy servo maps that crackled and creased and objected if a window was opened. With her glasses on, a barley sugar in her mouth, she would really try to understand what she was looking at, and if it was the right thing to be looking at, her heart racing harder the harder she stared. Her husband, watching the panic literally unfold, dealt with the situation by yelling: 'LEFT OR RIGHT?' He would decide on right, or left, even though she had not answered him. He would curse at left-hand lanes that disappeared and at unreadable signs and at crazy drivers, her poor mum quivering, glasses now a foggy inch from the map.

There were a lot of car rules: no music unless there was a straight stretch of at least half an hour, no eating, and no unscheduled stopping, ever, no matter what. *You meant to go to Perth and you're in Brisbane? No worries, just keep on Highway 1, maybe yell more loudly, but don't stop. Do the big lap.* Lou wondered if all the vans circumnavigating Australia were lost men refusing to stop.

On the many lengthy journeys she'd gone on as a child, from this aunt to that, from this base to that, Lou would always be perched in the middle of the backseat, on high alert to offer the driver bottled water and a barley sugar. She would rest one hand on her mother's shoulder. Occasionally, her mum would reach back and touch her fingers, tap, tap, tap, as if to say: *I love you, and I'm okay, I might even know where we are.*

But she didn't look okay when she arrived in Port Melbourne two years ago. Eighteen hours as navigator had made her pale. A huge map followed her out of the car. Lou's dad chased it, grabbed it, wiped the rain from it, and folded it in three perfect steps.

They were to stay overnight in Lou's apartment, then head off to Uncle Fred's birthday party the following morning. It was a terrible mistake. Her dad was tired and anxious and got grumpy because the food took ages. (*Ring the restaurant. Ring them again! Cancel the order. One star. No stars.*) He had never been violent, but his yelling had always scared her, and she was no longer as used to it as she had been. As they plated the noodles, she decided to ask her dad if he might consider going to the doctor about his anger issues and his OCD.

'What are you saying, that I'm crazy?' he'd said.

Crazy was not allowed, or even talked about, in the army/O'Dowd family. He laughed at the impossibility of it.

Him, crazy, when he'd driven all that way and paid a fortune for food that took two hours to arrive. He was not barking mad. He was right to be mad. And after all that they had given him the wrong noodles. Arseholes.

'You ever heard the saying: "If you keep meeting arseholes, chances are, you're the arsehole?"' Lou said.

He had not heard it and it was not the case. He met arseholes all day every day, sometimes the same ones, over and over.

This seemed very unlucky. And such a shame. A bit of Zoloft might have worked a treat for her dad, she reckoned, plus some counselling to undo all those military knots of his. She knew he was nice underneath. She'd experienced it as a kid: those father-daughter camping trips to Wilpena Pound; fishing on the Murray; hiking in the high country; building fires on Lake Eildon; falling asleep under the southern stars, survivors, together.

Her dad had stopped yelling about the noodles and was now eating them.

'I adore this place,' her mother said, sipping a glass of red on the balcony. 'But how can you afford it on your wages?'

'Thanks.' Lou did not want to answer the second question.

'You are still working at the café?' her dad said. He'd been nagging her for three years to get some direction; even offered to pay her fees if she enrolled to learn something useful.

'Yes,' she lied.

'Part time?'

'It varies.'

'And that's all?'

'Yes.'

'Are the wages good in sandwiches?'

'No.'

'You're twenty,' he said, preparing another mouthful of the wrong noodles.

'Twenty-one,' Lou said, annoyed enough to add: 'Actually my boyfriend pays for this flat.'

She had just estranged herself from her semi-Catholic, super-pious parents and she knew it. Fuck them.

'You've got a boyfriend? Where is he? So this is for the two of you?' Her mum gave her dad a look: *See, told you it'd all turn out all right.*

'He's married,' Lou said. 'I only have to see him twice a week.' Okay, so now it was definitely over. She would not be speaking to her parents again.

Her mother spewed out some red wine.

Her father turned as red as the Malbec, fist tightening around his glass. 'So you're a mistress.' Voice getting louder, almost yelling now. 'Is that what we say? Is that what we're supposed to tell people?'

Lou didn't care anymore. 'Tell them a man pays for my services, like you pay for mum's, tell them I'm a whore.'

Lou didn't go to Uncle Fred's the following day. She stopped going to family gatherings altogether. She made excuses at Christmas and at Easter and on birthdays. She didn't listen to her mother's voicemails and did not respond to her 'come home' texts. She talked to her new friends – she couldn't remember who – about how she'd gone no-contact because she'd finally realised that her father was a tyrant and that her mother was an idiot. 'I'm an orphan,' she said to a fabulous new friend in a Fitzroy bar one night. 'Why shouldn't I have a Daddy Warbucks?'

'Lou! Lou, here, it's me.'

It was her mum, in the check-in queue. Her silver hair was fabulous, but she looked about twenty years older than she did two years ago. 'Oh my god, Mum!' She had come to see her little girl off. She had come to surprise her after all.

'I've saved a spot for you. Come up here. Can you let my daughter through, please? Thank you. Can you move aside, please? Thank you.'

'Seriously?' said a young mother. Lou had just pushed past her toddler and made him cry.

'Sorry,' Lou said. She ducked under the barrier and

rolled her purple glitter suitcase (with the word *JUICY* written on it) all the way to her mum, ducking back underneath the barrier again and hugging her.

'Oh darling,' her mum said, a few times. She was dressed in her usual colourful comfort: soft pinks, flowing scarves, layers of lovely. She had a package and a beaming smile. 'Your dad and I are neck and neck,' she said, pointing to the queue adjacent.

'Hey Lou!' her father waved. He was directly opposite, in the other huge queue for Glasgow. 'Don't get too comfy,' he yelled (so loudly). 'I'm still betting on my queue. See that couple third from the front? They only have cabin bags, see.'

'Shh.' Her mother seemed to be on the lookout for the police or worse. The bubble-wrapped package in her hand was getting more suspicious by the minute.

'Those three,' her father said, 'see, with the thingy.' He pointed to his head.

'Shh,' Lou's mum said.

Her dad turned it down about half a notch. 'They only have five bags. UK passports, far as I can see.'

Oh god, he had to be shut up. Lou gave her dad the thumbs-up and spoke to her mum in a whisper. 'You drove all the way down?'

'Only from Hall's Gap. We've been camping.' Her mum was getting tearful, hugging a lot. 'I've missed you so much. I'm so happy to see you. I'm excited for you. Really proud.'

'I bet Dad's relieved I've got a proper job?' Lou said.

'Yes, we're both proud of you for that, and for being brave, aiming for better. He was not a good deal, that Alan Bainbridge. You can do better than that.'

Lou was getting tearful too, when her father yelled from his stagnant queue: 'The jam!'

'Oh yeah, I made you some apricot jam.' Lou's mum held out the large bubble-wrapped package she'd been clutching all this time. 'Have you got room?'

'Um.' No, Lou did not have room. 'Ah, let me see.' She knelt down and unzipped her suitcase, almost hitting a passenger's foot as it flipped open. Everyone around her shuffled to make space. The unzipped suitcase was making everything seem out of control. Lou pretended to look for space for the world's largest jar of apricot jam. 'I could swap it for the leather jacket?' Lou could not believe she'd said this. The jacket was Versace and went with everything.

'No, I'll just send this on in the post,' her mum said.

Lou was about to zip her case again.

'Or the jacket,' said her mum. 'It weighs less.'

It'd probably only take a week for a package to arrive. Lou could wait a week for the jacket.

Or for the *jam*.

'Girls!' It was her dad. 'Check it out,' he said. 'Told ya – check it out.' His queue was moving. He was already two places ahead. He moved forward another foot. 'Girls! Get here, come, come…'

Lou zipped her case as fast as she could. She and her mum ducked under the barrier and moved over to his queue, which kept moving all the way to the desk.

After scanning her boarding pass, Lou turned to wave goodbye. Her father had put his arm around her mother.

Her mother was now clutching the Versace leather jacket.

CHAPTER THREE

There was a party in the bulkheads. Naomi was heading to Dubai to make lots of money. Tahida and her mates were off to Greece. Gregor was going to Glasgow for his dad's funeral. He was assertive about ordering drinks, Gregor:

'You have to beg,' he said. 'Not like in the good old days of the Aeroflot milk run. Made some good mates on those flights: chain-smoked in the aisles, stuffed our faces, booze just kept on coming.'

The steward, face like fizz, handed Gregor another two G & Ts.

'We'll be needing another in twenty minutes,' he said, then cheered the late, great John Stewart McAveney. 'God rest his soul of gold. To my dad, a steadfast, loving father; a kind, generous husband; and a fucking great drinker.'

(Too great. It was his liver.)

Lou was on fire for the last few hours of the flight. Everything she said was clever and hilarious, like that story she told about that – what was it again? – Naomi peed and it went through to the seat. She had to borrow Lou's spare undies. Thanks to many tips from her father, she always packed an appropriate and perfect day bag.

'Lou O'Dowd,' Naomi had said, holding her stomach

with one hand, Lou's labelled Cat Woman pants with the other. They were her favourites since going thong tee-total. 'Who the fuck's gonna steal these?' she asked, still laughing.

'You,' Lou said, helping Naomi (plus wet patch) into the toilet.

Half an hour after landing in Dubai, she hugged her friends goodbye. They would connect online, keep in touch, never forget, they were the bulkhead crew, etcetera.

She needed sunglasses in Dubai's glaring gold transit terminal. Lou took them off to wash her face and brush her teeth in the ladies, then hovered around the comfy loungers until one became free. She needed painkillers. She needed food. She would drink nothing and eat everything on the next leg.

Gregor, greyer and fatter and less fabulous than she remembered, was in the seat behind her when she boarded the Glasgow flight. 'Why are you crying?' he asked.

'Am I?' She hadn't noticed. How embarrassing.

'Only way to deal with this is to keep going,' he said, demanding a pre-take-off round.

Lou took one sip, closed her eyes, and didn't wake till they landed in Glasgow. She'd missed all the meals; had never felt so ill.

At baggage reclaim, she told Gregor she'd love to visit him in 'the real Scotland', and maybe one day she would. He had a cabin on Loch Lomond, beautiful and secluded, perfect place to bury a body. Phew, that was her suitcase. She hugged her Glaswegian friend goodbye, made the usual promises, and headed out into the crisp, scentless Scottish air.

Someone was pricking her with a pin, she was shrivelling – she woke, it was the sound of the bus door opening. Lou had arrived in the most beautiful city in the world, although so far all she could see were buses … and Becks, at the exit, struggling to hold an enormous banner with *THE MAD KANGAROO* painted on it in thick purple.

Lou had spotted her little cousin's Edinburgh Festival posts on TikTok. They'd not spoken for two years, so as an olive branch (that might yield gold), Lou liked a few pictures, then messaged: *Hey Becks, loving your life! It's over with Alan btw. I'm coming to the UK … would love to see your play, it looks amazing. Send the link? x*

There she was in the bus terminal: Uncle Fred's baby girl, little Becks. Little Becks who could read at three and play the piano (badly and often) at seven and perform sonnets before important audiences at twelve and write boring, self-important shit at fourteen and keep doing it. She was looking so like her dad.

Uncle Fred and Lou's dad were mischievous when they were little – ran away from home on a makeshift raft one time, wandered off and got lost in the bush on a camping trip. There were a lot of stories, which were repeated by either one or the other of the brothers at each meeting. Lou was surprised she'd forgotten all but two of these tales. The brothers drifted apart when they became men – Fred increasingly suburban, corporate and jovial; her father stiff from army rules, which suited his temperament and which he applied to family life. Despite their growing differences, Lou and Becks continued to be thrown together for Christmas, Easter, special birthdays, weddings and, of course, the annual O'Dowd family picnic.

Becks was irritating as a child, but she became infuriating as a teenager. She started calling Lou 'The Mad Kangaroo', for example. Lou didn't know why and wished she would stop. At family gatherings, like at the last picnic in Nagambie, she always sat too close to Lou, talked for hours about literature and art, or whatever pretentiousness she'd learned about recently. Her face was only ever an inch away. If Lou moved back, she moved too. She ate what Lou ate, wore what she wore (or tried). She followed her around and asked question after question. ('Would a denim jacket like that suit me do you think? Can I try it on?') Even with hormones raging, she was full of excitement and optimism; brimming with the kind of fun ideas that bored and exhausted Lou – *Race you round the lake? Want to row out to the middle and dive off? Let's meet up when you're in Melbourne and go shopping – girls' day! Next picnic let's both bring our own baking. I'm having a party! Wanna go see* Les Mis?

Apart from her leech of a little cousin, Lou loved the annual family picnic in Nagambie. She had so many cool older cousins, all with a happier O'Dowd for a dad. They were kind to each other and intriguing. Some were from the eastern suburbs and went clubbing in the city, some were country bogans who could water-ski and fish (like Lou), some were doctors who knew about wine, and some were twins (well, two were). Lou wished she saw them for more than five hours a year and that she was allowed to do the things they did and eat the food they ate. The aunts always brought baskets filled with fairy cakes with real cream, fairy bread with real butter, pavlova with crushed-up peppermint crisp on top, homemade toffee – some chewy, some hard, some light, some dark – chocolate ripple cake, zucchini bread with walnuts. No-one bothered with savouries, except for Aunty Shirl, who brought the home-made sausage rolls. Lou always ate as much as she could stomach, careful her dad didn't see because almost everyone on his side of the family died of heart attacks in their sixties.

Lou's relationship with Becks was limited to family gatherings until they both moved to the same area as young adults. Lou, twenty-one, was in her glamorous love nest in Port Melbourne. Becks, nineteen, was in a shared flat in the neighbouring South Melbourne. They started going for morning beach swims together – once a week at first, then Becks suggested twice, then Becks suggested three times. They started having lunch occasionally. They began texting, chatting each day, telling each other secrets. It was the kind of buzzy chemistry Lou was used to with a bright new friendship: there was nothing more wonderful than connecting with someone whose stories you didn't know yet, who's never heard yours.

She'd never thought of Becks as a potential friend. She didn't think cousins qualified, especially grating little ones. They'd never pricked fingers and merged blood, or buried a precious box of memories to dig up at the age of fifty. But before she knew it, Becks was her new best friend.

She lied about Alan at first; told Becks he was her boyfriend and that they lived together. She must have known Becks would disapprove and was having too much fun to spoil the mood. The cousins got drunk at bars, had movie-and-munchie nights at Becks's flat, spent afternoons baking family recipes, evenings stuffing their faces with cakes and biccies. They went for swims, walks. They stayed up all night talking about their families and what they wanted to achieve. Becks wanted her play to do well, and also an Oscar, plus world peace. Lou wanted to go to Costa Rica and live in a cabin with a pool in the jungle and spear fish in the ocean for her breakfast. Costa Rica Lou was going to smile all the time, even in her sleep.

One day, sick of hanging at Becks's grotty bohemian flat, Lou decided to fess up. They'd be much more comfortable at her clean, gorgeous apartment. She gathered the courage after a swim. 'Alan doesn't live with me. He's married.'

Becks looked shocked; disappointed in her hero cousin. 'As long as you're happy. Are you happy?'

'Absolutely.' Lou was sick of people asking her that.

Becks came over to the penthouse for brunch the following morning with a bundle of prospectuses and the contact details for Jane at the Night Theatre. 'She's looking for someone at the box office,' Becks said.

'I'm not looking for work,' Lou said, trying to remain calm with this self-righteous, entitled, pain-in-the-arse kid. She'd had the argument so many times, mostly with herself. She could work at the café and get two other similar jobs. If she worked ninety hours a week, she could live like all the respectable people – there were so many of them – with their rental agreements and their car loans and bills and kids and horrible holidays. She could go back to school and try to get into nursing, like Jane from swimming, who paid off a credit card recently by selling her soiled undies online (picture of her dressed in her nurse's uniform – date stamped, undies partly visible – included in the price). Or she could study, study, study, enough to be a teacher, like the couple she lived with in Brisbane. After the studying, she could work one hundred hours plus a week, and be constantly on the brink of divorce, murder and/or suicide.

'You don't want a career?' said Becks.

Like her dad's? A trained, dedicated soldier hanging around, waiting for a fight; like a doctor waiting for a patient. For decades. No wonder he was angry.

Or she could get a career in finance, like Sharon Henderson had, which came as a big surprise to everyone in the Puckapunyal and Seymour area. (Sharon had kept all non-breast-related talent very well hidden.) Good on Sharon for getting a career, making a fortune, losing it, and killing herself. (Poor Sharon.)

Lou didn't know anyone with a 'career' who was happy, but she didn't want to say that. Instead, she made something up. 'I was thinking of being a personal trainer.'

Over the next few days, Becks checked in regularly – *Have you ended it yet? Did you send in that application? What about this course? Have you done it, have you done it?*

Lou did check out Becks's prospectuses. The courses sounded dull and were expensive. If she finished one, she'd owe a fortune. There were very few jobs anyway. And she wasn't into fitness. And the pay was rubbish. Rent was extortionate. She'd rather Alan. He was straight-forward and generous. Life was easy. It was a no-brainer.

Lou had to lie in the end. It was the only way to shut Becks up. If she had to listen to one more lecture about ambition and dreams and life being short and women helping each other.

'I have ended it,' Lou announced at a post-swim brunch. 'It's over.'

Staff and customers watched as Becks jumped from her seat, squealing, then hugged and kissed her friend. 'Sorry everyone,' she announced. 'It's just that my big cousin has finally ended a horrible, exploitative relationship.'

Two people clapped. One was the owner. 'This is on the house,' she said.

To celebrate, Becks dragged Lou around the best boutiques in Chapel Street and made her try on more than a dozen outfits. She filmed it too, a montage scene. 'It's a big day,' Becks said. 'New Lou needs a new wardrobe.' She insisted on paying for everything because Lou would need to budget from now on. She'd need a cheaper place to live – Becks could help her look for one, maybe Frankston? And at least one job, of course, especially if she was paying for some kind of tech qualification, which she really should.

When she got home, Lou put her shopping bags on the sofa, poured herself a gin and tonic, and muted Becks on every platform. It had been fun, but it was over. Far easier to end a friendship with a woman than to maintain it, especially Becks, fuck's sake.

The view! She lived like a movie star. She didn't need Becks to hang out with. She'd met a few fun women on the morning swims. She might suggest a drink with one of them. As she watched the colours of the city change, she relaxed. It had been an adventure, but it was intense. So much chatting, so many activities, hardly any time alone. She could never have kept that up.

Two days later, Becks ambushed her on the beach.

'Why are you ghosting me?'

'I'm not.'

'You're still with him?'

'No. Yeah, Jesus. You're so judgemental.' And so clingy, and so needy, and so close-up, all the fucking time.

'I am judging you about this,' Becks said. 'If you ever manage to get away from him, let me know.' She walked off, so superior.

'My beautiful cuz!' Lou said, dumping her suitcase and running towards Becks with open arms. 'I have missed you so much.' She meant it too. It was so good to hug her friend. 'Have you missed me?'

'Life's not as much fun without you. I mean, it's still fun, but not *as*.'

'You missed me,' said Lou, going in for a second hug. 'You love me, you're really glad I'm here.'

CHAPTER FOUR

Becks didn't need fashion advice anymore. She was almost intimidating. They were going to have the greatest adventures together, be the closest of friends.

'You stink of booze,' Becks said.

'There was a party on the plane.' Lou was regretting her last three drinks, as well as giving her spare pants to an alcoholic stranger.

'What are you gonna do when it's free?' Becks said. 'Stomach up, though, you've arrived in party town. Follow me – sorry, need to hurry. You should get some sleep. Don't worry about coming today, come another day.'

Becks was starring in a play that Lou knew nothing about and had no interest in. Another wave of nausea came over her, a memory of something terrible – that she may have promised to come to the play as soon as she got off the plane. It sounded like the kind of promise Lou would make. Theatre, no, no, no, altogether too risky. What had she done, what had she said? She remembered now. She had posted something idiotic on Insta (*Can't wait to see this – soon as I arrive!).*

'You kidding?' Lou said. 'I'm coming. I might vomit at you though.'

'Don't worry, people have been doing way worse than that.'

Becks held the banner in the air all the way past the Georgian townhouses on the grey streets, one of which was Nevis Place, where Lou would be working.

Lou had Google-walked around the city many times – each time she was immersed in a gothic-fantasy video game. She could walk everywhere; see its edges. Man had filled each inch centuries ago; left no space to ruin. It would always look like Edinburgh. Never like Melbourne, never like any other city. In real life, Edinburgh was just as dreamlike; The Land of All That Is Pretty at the top of The Magic Faraway Tree. Did people actually live here – did *she*? – in this winding world of stones and princesses?

The Airbnb was two streets further down the hill from Nevis Place, so handy. On the way, Becks bumped into four people she knew, exchanging flyers with two of them.

'Small town,' Becks said.

Lou's arms shuddered as the suitcase bounced over cobbles and pavements, weaving past shoppers and coffee-goers, none of whom seemed to notice the purple banner. There were too many other weird signs in the Edinburgh air, too many other mad kangaroos.

'Home sweet home,' said Becks. The right-hand side of the cobbled street was lined with stern stone terraces, the left with three-storey Georgian tenement flats, black criss-crosses on the windows. It was sunny but Lou had a confusing shiver that was either euphoria or a chill from being encased in stone. This was where Lou was going to live – in this ancient, man-made place where there was nothing ugly, not one thing, and where nothing was out of place.

'Hope you're fit,' Becks said, opening the blue arched door leading to the shared stairway. 'We're at the top.'

Banner and baggage in hand, Becks bounced up two steps at a time. Lou ambled as she took in the worn flagstones, the tiled walls, the twirling cast-iron banister and the stained-glass skylight. She was Rapunzel heading to her tower.

'Come on, come in,' Becks said, opening the door and giving her a quick tour of the flat with its oak floors and ornate ceiling roses.

'This is you.' Becks opened the door to the front bedroom. There was a long-haired man lying on one of the twin beds. He had headphones on. 'This is Cam from Canberra.'

'Hi Cam.' His hand was as sticky as Lou feared.

'Cam was paying eighty quid a night sharing a campervan,' Becks said, 'way out Woop Woop, where there are no street signs and all the shops are boarded up. Hope you don't mind. It's impossible for performers these days.'

That's right, Becks saved people. There were always at least four randoms dossing in her South Melbourne house. She was constantly organising events that required a twenty-dollar donation and a level-one excuse to get out of (Covid, dead dog). When Becks went out in Melbourne, she'd take a bag of two-dollar coins and wouldn't pass a homeless person without a conversation and a contribution. After a while, Lou always booked taxis when they went out together.

'You're a performer?' Lou said, but Cam's earphones must have been noise-cancelling.

Becks brandished a flyer she grabbed from the pile in the corner – *Cam Says* – and chuckled at the underweight, unwashed man whose depression was thickening the air.

Lou put her jacket and the flyer on the single bed closest to the window and stopped herself from screaming. Rapunzel didn't share her tower with a homeless guy.

'You really want to come?' Becks yelled from her bedroom.

No, Lou thought, opening the curtain and gasping at the view, but there was no way to get out of this. 'Love to,' she yelled. Jesus Christ, this city hurt her eyes. *What was that hill, what was that tower, what were those ruins, was that the castle?*

'Need to head in five, that okay?'

Lou opened the window and squeezed her head out just in time to projectile vomit. Her insides made it halfway across the street before raining on the cobblestones three storeys below. Two heaves and several slow breaths later, she pulled her head back in to find Cam staring at her in disgust.

❁

Becks had to run ahead when they reached the top of Broughton Street. 'Chips with curry sauce and Irn-Bru,' she said, 'you'll feel good as new.' Lou watched as her cousin jogged up the hill with sporty efficiency, high-fiving an elderly woman without stopping ('Hey, Nora'), and depositing a coin into someone's cup.

Lou put the crazy location into her phone: *The Caves, Cowgate.*

By the time she got to the North Bridge she had managed one orange-coated chip and one inscrutable orange sip. She threw the lot in a bin and shuffled her way through the thick crowds, seeing nothing but her feet.

Cowgate deserved its name and so did The Caves. She'd made it just in time, but had to elbow her way into the venue, past people dressed in furry animal suits and women holding banners saying stuff like *Avenge Sylvia.* The theatre was about a quarter full, shame. There was only one aisle seat, which happened to be two seats from the only man in the audience. Lou took the aisle seat, put her head between her legs and breathed slowly, a half-chewed curried chip firmly lodged in the back of her throat. The smell of the guy beside her was easing her nausea. Oops, he caught her sniffing.

'Sandalwood,' he said in an English accent. 'Birthday present.'

'Is it your birthday?' she asked.

He shook his head, wasn't after small talk.

Lou assumed he was a professional of some sort, a reviewer perhaps. He was dressed in designer jeans, crisp shirt and a cashmere jumper. He had a rich person's hair: unkempt, why should he care. He sat up straight as if he was about to ask a question. He wore a Gucci watch, shiny black Saint Lauren Derbies. It was very shallow to be attracted to designer shoes and wealthy hairdos, but she was immediately interested in the man sitting next to her. She could feel it, like she did with Alan, who had been wearing his Armani watch when she met him.

The lights went down. There was no time to chat up sandalwood guy. Lou became overwhelmed with dread at what she was about to endure. *Plath! The Musical.* She detested poems and musicals. She'd have to work out what to say to Becks after, something about the enthusiastic audience maybe, or the eerie, vaulted venue. The curtains opened onto a stage that was set in a fifties kitchen. An apron-clad woman was stirring something over the cooker, a little angrily it seemed. She'd tell Becks she loved the costumes and the set design, Lou decided, rocking her head on the seat in front of her, back and forth, back and forth, in time with the beat of spoon against saucepan … *boom, boom, boom, boom…*

She woke to clapping. Becks and the cast made a final bow on stage. The curtains closed, the lights went up.

'I cannot believe you slept through that,' sandalwood guy said.

'Was it good?'

He leaned in: 'Wish I'd slept through it.'

Sandalwood guy, otherwise known as Timothy, couldn't get enough of Lou in the foyer. No wonder, she was even funnier than she had been on the plane.

'So, what is it you're wearing?' he asked, leaning in for a sniff.

'I'm wearing the farts of two hundred long-haul passengers.'

There was a spark, perhaps several, until her cousin bounced over for a squeal and a hug.

'Congratulations, that was amazing. This is Timothy,' Lou said.

'Hello Timothy. I saw you next to my jetlagged' – she made a snoring sound – 'cousin.'

'I'm sorry,' Lou said. 'I'll come again.' *Why, why, why did she say that?*

'Yes, you shall,' Becks said. 'So Timothy, are you a journalist?'

'No.'

'Just a man on his own?'

'Yes.'

'At *Plath! The Musical*?'

'That's right.'

'You like Sylvia Plath?'

'Of course.'

'And musicals?'

'Interesting you call it a musical.'

'Is it?'

'I suppose it depends on your definition of music.'

'Mm hmm,' said Becks. 'And you like matinees?'

'I'm a huge fan of matinees,' Timothy said. 'People aren't supposed to be so raw in the middle of the afternoon. There's something intimate about it, voyeuristic even. Well done, by the way, it was … thought-provoking.'

'Which thought did it provoke?'

Becks seemed to have taken against him. Annoying.

'I admire your attempt to reframe the musical theatre genre to subvert stereotypical patriarchal tropes of performative femininity and how you create a radical new and affective form of *unheimlich* musical theatre that utilises Plath's iconic status ironically to explore a contemporary acknowledgement of toxic masculinity's gaslighting.' Tim needed to take a breath.

'Nice,' Lou said, not really listening or understanding, but very pleased that he could spar with Becks and win.

'You read the blurb,' Becks said. 'You have a decent memory. I'm not buying you. I'd say there's a sixty-percent chance you're here to chat up women. What are you going to see tomorrow?'

'The monologue, two doors down.'

'You mean the play about endometriosis?'

'Maybe.'

'Ninety-five percent.'

Lou wanted her cousin to shut up. She didn't care if he was a player.

'Gotta go,' Becks said. 'The *Telegraph* and the *Guardian* want to talk to me, can you believe it. Pub later?'

'If I don't get some sleep I'll die,' Lou said. 'Rain check?'

She was alone in the foyer with Timothy now. Hmm, should she? She sniffed her underarm when he wasn't looking. Not great. She was wearing three-day-old underpants. Her breath smelt of vomit. Her socks smelt of urine. Oh well, she'd find another sandalwood guy. His sentences were too long anyway. Time to shower, time for bed. 'Nice to meet you,' she said, heading out the door. He was probably looking at her – she didn't turn to check.

She found herself in The Meadows and weaved her way through happy gatherings to a quiet stretch of grass. She did a three-sixty, arms outstretched. A group of old people was playing rounders. Someone was juggling. A family was picnicking, tossing a ball to a dog. She skipped along the grass once, twice. She spun, she smiled.

She fainted, woke with a clown and two children looking at her.

'Are you okay?' said the clown.

'I am, sorry,' said Lou, sitting, then standing, then giving a little wave to the audience she hadn't realise she'd attracted.

To her surprise, the chip shop beckoned her on the way home.

'Hungry again?' said the woman behind the counter. 'It's Lou isn't it, Becks's cousin? She's gorgeous, that girl. Salt and sauce with that?'

She shovelled it all in on the way home. Chips and curry sauce (salt, no sauce) and a can of Irn-Bru, Take Two. Who knew?

The depressed comedian was lying on his bed again, fully clothed, earphones in, staring at the ceiling. She set herself up like she always did in every new room she moved to: with her thin pillow and its ripped cotton case, daisies and *Little Lou* embroidered on it (fifth birthday, from her mum); her framed photo of the family boat in Holland's Landing, parents and Lou and a large bream on board; and the shredded pink blanket she used to suck as a toddler, frayed, half its original size. She unpacked her mum's homemade apricot jam and put it in the fridge with a note: *Help yourselves, roomies, with love from Mummy O'Dowd xxx*

In her little bed, she clutched her blanky, wrapped her head in her thin pillow and fantasised about outdoor sex with pretty sandalwood guy: *We're in a car, Tim and I. No, we're on a country walk. No, we're in a walled garden. I can feel the Edinburgh air on my legs and bum. I only know it's Timothy back there because of the smell of sandalwood.*

CHAPTER FIVE

She woke at 3.05pm the next day to a message from Becks on her phone. Another poor Aussie performer had moved in overnight.

'Hope you don't mind. She was paying 120 quid a night to share with two bossy old women in Morningside. She's so talented.'

Performer number two had set up camp on the sofa in the living room. She was at least eighty years old and relentlessly chatty: with thoughts she must convey about Dubai airport, Waverley Station, the water pressure and if she'd had her special pill yet ('the time difference makes it all very confusing'). The place was a pigsty, stuff everywhere. Lou tried not to see it, but her face was boiling and the shuddering was starting in her chest. She probably looked exactly like her dad did when he encountered an arsehole. She'd tell him to take time out. He'd tell her to shut the fuck up. She found herself power walking to The Caves. The endometriosis matinee should just about be winding up. She waited in the foyer as the audience poured out, and sure enough, there was Sandalwood, chatting to a bleached soccer mum in her late thirties. The two of them headed for the bar. Soccer mum bought two glasses of wine, which sandalwood nursed while she went to powder her nose.

'Gotcha,' Lou said, sitting beside him.

'You got me?' Timothy finished his wine then started on soccer mum's. 'You knew I was going to be here. What a brazen girl you are.' He sniffed. 'Smelling better today. Have you eaten?'

Soccer Mum was heading back to the bar. 'I'm not paying for your lunch,' Lou said.

Timothy grabbed her hand and hauled her outside, leaving Soccer Mum to shake her head and sigh, *I am a fuckwit. How can I still be so stupid?*

They began walking together, not knowing where they were going. 'You're not buying me lunch either,' Lou said.

'Why's that?'

'If you buy me lunch, I'll owe you.'

'What will you owe me?'

'Depends what's for lunch.'

They did a Greggs crawl of the city, taking turns to buy sausage rolls, chicken bakes, fudge doughnuts, pineapple tarts and yum yums. She loved how much he ate. He said they'd walk it off. They explored the Old Town, the New Town, the villagey town, the royal yacht town, crawling into a bar every hour or so for a beer or a cocktail. Lou managed to feign interest in Timothy's endless facts about architecture until 8.30pm. 'Shut up,' she said, putting her finger on his lips. 'Let's fuck in a lane.'

'Can we not go to yours?' Tim said, following her lead.

'Things always get too serious indoors,' Lou said, dragging him into a small, dingy laneway.

'Hang on, not here,' Tim said, pointing to the CCTV camera. 'It's an ugly charge, getting caught for this. Or do you like getting caught?'

'No! Certainly not by the police,' Lou said, resting her back against the graffitied wall of the bin-filled lane. 'I just have a thing for outdoor sex.'

It started with Haz, her boyfriend from the age of fifteen to seventeen. Lou's parents wouldn't let Haz come over, and she wasn't allowed to visit his place, so they were forced to go al fresco and left their scent all over Puckapunyal. It was daring, passionate, teenaged sex: in the pool changing rooms, behind trees, in bushes, by the river on a blanket, on the river in a boat, in his dad's car, in his mum's pottery shed, on the climbing frame and on the swing and on the roundabout, sometimes all three, a sexual obstacle course. Lou was sick with love for Haz. They could talk for hours, kiss for longer. They got drunk and smashed things up together, they made prank calls. Lou didn't need anyone other than Haz – lucky, as she'd only made one friend in Puckapunyal, and she didn't like her.

It ended one Saturday night in the McDonald's at

Seymour when Haz's mate's sister said: 'So you're gonna do long distance?'

'Yeah,' Lou said. Her dad was moving them to a new base, this one in Queensland. But yeah, she and Haz were in love and were going to do long distance till school was done: the missing, the phone calls, the heart growing fonder, the writing of love messages, maybe even letters, the anticipation of romantic Sydney rendezvous.

'Y'know he roots Sharon Henderson, yeah, down by the creek?'

'Yeah,' Lou had said, her face beating with heat. She had been right all along to dislike Sharon Henderson, with her built-in trampoline; her jacuzzi that was always full and hot; and cool parents who were never around.

Lou couldn't get home fast enough. She had loved and lost for many years by then. Friend after friend after non-friend, bad birthday party after bad birthday party. Aged six, for example, after moving to a base in WA, her mother organised a pyjama princess party with makeup and dress-ups and movies and sweet popcorn. No-one showed. The following two parties were even worse. The girls who showed were dweebs and/or ugly, and they wouldn't get out of Lou's bedroom. After the age of six, Lou's guest lists were worrying and shameful. Five friends at most, none of whom liked her much, and vice versa. And it could be guaranteed that none of them would like each other. She stopped having parties at the age of eleven but hadn't trusted friends for several years before then.

Sharon Henderson. They slept over at each other's all the time. They went to Melbourne on the train, twice, they hung out in the park, played softball, went swimming.

When Lou got home, she locked herself in the bedroom to cry. Well, not locked. Her mum and dad wouldn't let her do that, but they respected it when she turned the sign on her door to *Please Do Not Disturb*.

She was so glad that Haz had never been in her room. Sharon Henderson had though, ugh. She ripped the photos of Sharon and Haz from the wall until it was a safe place again. Her place, the same four walls she occupied no matter what base she was on, no matter what box-house she was in. Her bed, her clothes and shoes (on display), her makeup, her blanky, her pillow, her desk, her laptop. She could be naked all day in this space. She could dance, and really try to be great at it. She could sing (ditto). She could write party lists and scribble them out again. She could cry. She liked to cry. If she felt like groaning while crying, she could do that too. She would never let anyone in her room again (except her mother for washing and sheets and meals, and her father if something broke or if she had a question about ferrets or fossils).

After a focused howl, she forgot all about Haz and Sharon Henderson. Another betrayal – whatever, move on.

In fact, she was moving on, to Queensland, where it was beautiful one day and perfect the next. She'd surf in Queensland, she'd ride waves and have a tan and go shopping in bathers with a friend called Millie. She had packing to do. Excellent, she loved packing.

She hadn't helped her dad with the big moves for many years. Seven apparently. 'You stopped asking me,' she said.

'You started being an absolute pain in the arse,' he said.

'Did I?'

'The great trampoline tantrum of 2013 ring a bell?'

It didn't really. Oh hang on. She might have sooked about her trampoline. She did love it more than anything she had ever loved. In fact, she probably hadn't loved anything as much since. She could bounce on it, do tricks, sunbathe, have picnics, entice potential friends. It was the private garden attached to her private bedroom. 'You sold it without telling me,' she said.

'It was for under-twelves,' he said, not stopping the three things he was doing, all of them well. 'Now are you going to sook all day about bouncy toys or are you going to be useful?'

'Useful.'

'Good, you're on your bedroom, kitchen and living room. The colour codes are all on the wall, materials in the shed. You're going to do this? You're going to focus?'

'I am,' Lou said. 'But can I moan, if I've earned it, like, once an hour?'

'Only if you've been stabbed.'

For the following week, Lou lost herself in her father's meticulous, exceptional systems, wrapping things in certain materials in a certain way, putting certain things in certain boxes in a certain way, labelling certain things in certain places with certain pens. She put Haz in one of those boxes, taped him up nice and tight.

The lane wasn't as quiet as they'd expected. She and Tim were behind a huge recycling bin and had to stop and play dead twice while smoking restaurant staff exited metal doors to smoke in the squalor. They giggled the first time, Tim's mouth over Lou's. They resumed when the chef went back into his kitchen. They kept quiet (but didn't stop) for the waitress, who came out a moment later.

Thank god and what a relief. It had been too long since she'd had sex the only way she liked it: no beds, no housemates and no doors.

At sixteen, Lou left the family home and moved to Brisbane. She shared a flat with three teachers from the UK, one of whom had a teenaged son.

At last, she could put a lock on the door. She sighed with relief when she stepped inside, giggled when she got into her bed and enveloped her head. She was happy in Brisbane. She nabbed a part-time job in a fancy restaurant, got huge tips and a sore face from smiling. She made great friends – Desire and Pop – who she lost touch with (oops, Pip). It must have been the sun that caused her to slip and allow a Tinder date into her room.

He wouldn't leave when she asked nicely a polite amount of time after sex. He was too tired. He was asleep, dribbling on the pillow she had dragged from house to house since she was a child. Eventually she called a taxi and woke him with a treat to ease the blow.

After that, Lou doubled down on her no-bedroom rule.

It was during the Brissie flat share that Lou decided she would never have children who would one day turn into teenagers, be a teacher, or do anything that involved being trapped in one room, or even in one building, all day. Her flatmates were the unhappiest people she had ever met. They would have cried all the time – if only they had the time.

In Sydney, she worked in a bar with two Canadians and lived in a brick house with a couple who had Zoom marriage-counselling three times a week in the open-plan kitchen/living room. (The wife needed help with her paranoia. The husband needed help with groping flatmates.) They had 'sex dates', this couple – every Friday evening Lou was to make herself scarce while the wife drank enough wine to endure a jack-rabbiting that went on for an hour and a half. Lou's headphones did not cancel the yelps of the poor woman who was stuck there, on that bed, under that man, all that time.

Before meeting Alan, Lou only had one romantic encounter in Melbourne, with Billy the bike-maintenance guy. They'd cycle somewhere remote, do it on the grass. It was fun but she always ended up with rashes and she didn't like cycling. She was glad to be distracted by dapper, older Alan Bainbridge, who walked into the café one morning with his fancy watch and his intense interest in her, and in her uniform. Lou's boss, Mick: fifty-five, Bali teeth, cunt, made her wear a tight, short, pink number with buttons all the way up the front. He gave her the daily task of organising the low cupboards, which required a lot of bending down.

'Get right in there,' he'd say. 'That's it, all the way to the back, further, further.'

She could almost smell his semi.

The uniform made her look like a nurse – apt, as the coffee was like hospital coffee. The uniform must have caught the eye of Alan Bainbridge, who slapped his hands on the counter, clocked her nametag (*LOU*), and said: 'Well, hello there, Lou-ise, is it?'

That's when she should have said: *NO. Lou, I'm Lou.*

'What a beautiful day. What sort of coffee do you use?'

'Shit coffee,' she said, leaning over the counter to whisper and sniff his aftershave (lemongrass): 'Everything here is pretty shit.'

'Shit coffee is exactly what I'm after,' he said. 'Full-fat milk, two sugars. And two sandwiches with the chicken breast and apricot curry sauce, and salad but no beetroot. On the thinly sliced dark rye, with butter on both please. Oh and a piece of banana cake, the middle piece, ooh yeah that one. And two of the salted caramel brownies, and these.' He put two bottles of sparkling water on the counter and watched as she started the order.

'You on the lunch round today?' she said, spreading the apricot curry sauce.

'No, just for me,' he said.

Lou made a piggy sound and cut diagonally through the dark rye with her hefty sandwich knife.

He ordered the same thing at the same time every day from then on. 'One Alan?' she'd say, and he'd nod.

She liked that he was more than twice her age, that he wore expensive suits, had a naughty smile. There was sexual chemistry, and she believed they had great conversations. Looking back on it now, she realised they only ever talked about food, mainly apricot curry sauce. (The recipe was her boss, Mick's, secret.) Alan owned the café, all the office units above, the lot. Lou began to wear mascara and perfume. She started giving Alan a scoop and a half of shredded chicken per sandwich and she divulged one ingredient of the magic sauce (apricot jam). After a fortnight's flirting, she met him for dinner in Fitzroy. He paid, dropped her home, they did it in the car.

He loved it outside too. She had met the man of her Melbourne dreams.

Another fortnight later, she giggled her way through Alan's usual order, then watched her *boyfriend* walk out the door. By then, they'd done it in toilets, on back beaches, in carparks and on golf courses. She didn't question it. Why wouldn't he love it?

'You know he's married, yeah?' Mick said.

'Yeah.' The fire in her face was probably not invisible.

'The wife's a formidable fucker.'

She withheld her tears through the lunch rush then ran all the way home to her hovel in St Kilda.

So, you're married, she texted. *I suppose this is a burner phone, is it?*

He was typing … The dots were giving her hope.

…I thought you knew, sorry. Yes, it is a burner phone. Can we meet at 8, La Fiorentina?

No, she replied, deleting his number, determined to forget it. He was married. She wasn't a girlfriend. She was a fuckwit.

She didn't go to work for two weeks, stayed in bed mostly, did some yoga, bashed at the punch bag in the courtyard as her gormless unemployed stoner housemates commentated through interminable giggles. She cleaned and tidied for days and no-one thanked her enough. Three of them didn't even notice. She put systems in place for food storage and waste disposal, and both had gone to hell in a day. If she straightened something or made a suggestion her housemates would roll their eyes, like she was the weird one, being so neat and tidy. *Wtf is wrong with Lou?*

Everyone was relieved when Lou went back to work.

She'd hoped Alan might get his lunch elsewhere, but he came in at the same time as usual. She didn't say 'One Alan?' She moved to the other end of the counter, hoping to take someone else's order.

'Hi Louise,' he said. 'Can I get the usual, please?'

'Of course,' she said, taking two slices of white bread, buttering one side only, depositing a stingy scoop of shredded chicken and a thin slivering of apricot curry sauce.

'I miss you,' he said.

At least two customers heard. Mick too.

Lou wrapped a stale end piece of banana cake, bundled the order in a plastic bag and took payment.

He leaned in before leaving. 'La Fiorentina at eight,' he said.

⁂

When she got home, the entire ground floor of the hovel was scattered with shoes. There must have been hundreds of them. None of them seemed to match. A bucket bong marathon had turned the living room into a hotbox. In the kitchen, the sink and every countertop was covered with dirty dishes and bits of rotten animal.

She was starving. She had absolutely no money. She could really go for a risotto.

Lou arrived at the restaurant before Alan, ordered the 76 Saint-Emilion. Hair, makeup, outfit – it had never come together so well.

'I assumed you knew I was married,' Alan said before his bum hit the chair.

His timing and his honesty made it very difficult for her to throw her wine over his crisp white shirt. Of course she should have known. Why else did they do it in the car?

Alan got down to business over his caprese, starting with compliments. She had never looked more beautiful. He never stopped thinking about her. He missed her, loved her, needed her. She was lots of shiny things and deserving of the same. The necklace caught her hair when he put it on.

Over risotto, he laid out the terms and conditions, rightly confident that she was listening. He was never going to leave his wife. They'd been taking too many risks. He would move her into one of the vacant flats in Port Melbourne.

'I want a balcony,' Lou said.

He would attend the apartment on Tuesdays and Thursdays from 7-10pm. Three hours, twice a week. The bills would be included, plus an allowance of six thousand dollars a month.

'Nine thousand,' she'd said.

After a brief negotiation, they settled on eight.

It was a good deal. The penthouse would be her own for all but six hours a week, that's six hours out of 168. The rest of the time – 162 hours to herself – she could do whatever she wanted: reorganise the furniture, frame art, go swimming, eat out, go shopping. Her mother didn't have as much money, time, or fun as that. Nor did any other straight, attached woman that she knew, like Frankie Hillington who was a single mother now (ha) of two snotty kids (ha), one with health issues (not ha, obviously, that would be bad).

It was an amazing deal. They shook on it over limoncello and she left the hovel the following day.

The only problem was this: all sex would now be in the bedroom.

No problem, she could un-Alan the bedroom after his visits, after all. She could even sleep on the linen modular in the living area if she wanted, and deep-clean and close off the bedroom altogether. Shame though, with its panoramic beach + city views + wrap-around balcony. But there was a wider, north-facing balcony off the living room. She could doze off there to the eighty-inch screen on the wall and the heatless fake fire, which she couldn't turn off. She could handle this whole bedroom-sex thing, no problems. It was for Alan, after all, and she loved Alan. Alan said she was different from every other girl, woman. He thought she was fascinating – hard to work out, but worth it. He said she was spirited, adventurous, that he was seeing colour again. Alan really thought about the gifts he gave her, didn't try and do better than the links she sent via text. Even Haz had been difficult about gifts, insisting on choosing something himself, like the wrap-around skirt he had hunted for, apparently, in Seymour, obviously. If ever Alan did stray from her lists, he had personal shoppers to do the choosing and they were good. If a large, flat box arrived at her door, she knew she was about to look better than she ever had before. Imagine knowing her style and her size so well, dear, dear Alan ('s assistants).

She could do this. She could have Alan in her room for six hours a week. Anyway, he wouldn't be in the room most of the time. He'd be in the living area, on the balcony, doing all the pre stuff they did, like gift-giving (say thirty minutes), dinner (say sixty minutes), drinks and cocaine, depending, (around eighty minutes) and dancing (Lou only, around ten minutes). The bed part never lasted long. Alan's penis was too old and too large to fill with blood and required Viagra to get going. He liked her to watch it get hard, so she would huddle over his stomach as the turd-like object twitched once or twice before thickening and bouncing less impressively than his proud smile would indicate.

Even with the Viagra, Alan couldn't have sex for long, or he didn't want to. Either way, it was good news. He had seemed quite normal when they were sneaking around, doing it on back beaches, but he wasn't normal in bed. He didn't have to be. In the early, outdoor days he'd climax while saying, 'Don't move, don't move.' She didn't realise at the time how much he meant this. He wanted Lou to be a corpse for the duration. If she so much as scratched her nose he would take longer than seven minutes, so she never did. It wasn't too difficult. Alan was a gentle necrophile.

Lust disappeared after they moved sex inside, and love followed suit, but she didn't mourn for long. She threw herself into leisure and stuff, lots of stuff. It really was a very good deal.

But how she had missed the great outdoors! At last, with Tim, in that grotty cobbled lane, she was fulfilled again, having the time of her life, on her terms, in the most beautiful city in the world.

CHAPTER SIX

After the great lane shag, Lou walked Tim to the station. He had to go home to a made-up town called Linlithgow to do a made-up job called Asia Pacific Futures Broker, a night gig which apparently involved moving money from one side of a virtual table to the other.

'Send me a pic,' he said, numbers now exchanged.

'As if.' She often worried about the photos and videos that Alan had taken. He promised to delete them, but she could never be certain. What if Frieda found them one day, or their children? Thank god she was never going to have any children of her own. ('Is this you on the internet Mummy?') She wouldn't do the photo thing again, no way.

The next day they watched three comedy shows, one of them all the way to the end. They wandered the streets, gathered flyers, enjoyed street performers, ate from kiosks, snogged like teenagers in parks, chain-smoked rollies outside pubs.

He told her about his love of horse-riding and banjo and maths.

She told him she went spear fishing and rabbiting all the time as a kid with her sergeant-major father. 'You've got to get in position, Lou.' She was mimicking his gravelly Aussie accent. 'And when it's time, focus, fo…cus … and go.' Lou acted out spearing a fish with a little too much gusto.

'That sounds special,' he said.

'When I got older it was SOOOO boring. Same thing every time. We packed for days, drove for hours, unpacked for hours, made fire, made toilet, made water, made food, cleared up, made food, cleared up, made food, cleared up. I pretended to get lost at Holland's Landing, but I wasn't, I was running away.'

'My parents are dead,' he said. 'Boating accident. I don't like fishing either.'

She told him she was sorry then drank some more and told him about Haz cheating on her.

He told her about his first and only love, Tanya, married now, two children.

She told him about all the friends she'd ever made – how they all betrayed her or forgot about her. She was seven when her first and last BFF broke her heart. Frankie Hillington, with her amazing blood-swapping rituals and her pinky promises.

'See you at Easter,' little Frankie had said, sobbing by the expertly packed O'Dowd car and trailer. Her pinky held on until it caught the passenger window. As promised, Frankie messaged every day for two weeks, then never again. Lou heard on the grapevine that she very quickly became best friends forever with Binky McGill. They both loved table tennis, apparently. And Lady Gaga. From then on, Lou understood that friends were never best and never forever. They were romances – tingly and manic to begin with, with a shelf life of two years at most, at which point it would be clear that neither party loved table tennis nor Lady Gaga.

Lou confessed she'd not met many nice men: Haz, Creepy Mick at the café, Alan. She couldn't stop talking, letting it all out as she always did in new relationships. She told him about falling out with her parents, feeling shame. Honestly, she'd never been so interesting – just twenty-three, so far away, with nothing to hide and so much to say. She showed him the reference Frieda had given her, and a short (and carefully edited, no bits) sex tape, the only one that she kept – to remind herself that her relationship with Alan was not perfect. In the film, Alan was making love to corpse Lou. 'Can't believe I did that,' she said. 'But hey, that reference, that attempt at revenge, got me the perfect job, so go fuck yourself, Frieda.'

They were in the camera obscura now, looking at miniature people on a stone table. 'Feels like I've been telling you about someone else, not me. Like it's all just made-up,' she said.

'It's called dissociative disorder,' Timothy said.

'What's that?'

'Kinda means you compartmentalise, and you run away from pain.'

'Running away's better than leaning in.' She decided to change the subject. Talking about pain wasn't fun, and hers was minor compared to the loss of his parents. She wouldn't even describe any of her past experiences as painful. 'What's the worst thing you've ever done?' she said as they headed back out onto the Royal Mile.

'I headbutted someone once, broke his nose.'

This turned her on so much that she was pinned against a brick garage ten minutes later. At 9pm, she put her Wonder Woman pants in his pocket and waved him off at Waverley. She floated back to the flat, high on sandalwood guy. He lived in a place called Linlithgow, for fuck's sake; he made lots of money moving money around; he played the banjo; he never said 'don't move' or made her go to bed.

She unlocked the blue arched door and stepped into the shared stairwell. It was true that she was brazen. Pulling her T-shirt over her head she pointed her phone at her torso and clicked. A door opened, she heard a cough. T-shirt back in its rightful place, Lou realised a displeased woman was standing in front of her – the owner of ground left, no doubt, as her door was wide open. 'Hello,' Lou said.

'No tit pics in the close please,' the stiff woman said, slamming her enormous door.

A message pinged when Lou reached the top:

Holy shit, you are breathtaking. I think I really like you… T x

I think you really like me too, she replied, rummaging in her pockets and bumbag for her keys. She must have dropped them downstairs when she was doing soft porn. She heard buzzers buzzing at the outside entrance. The front door slammed and echoed up the tiled close. As she walked down the spiral stairs, she spotted a figure heading up. He was in between the ground and the first floor. She was on the third by now. It looked like a man. She wondered if he'd seen her keys, or picked them up. Lou coughed, she didn't want to scare him if they collided on the second floor. She coughed again, loudly this time, expecting to see him any moment. But he had turned around. He was heading downstairs. He was going back outside. The door slammed shut again. Perhaps he'd forgotten to get milk.

Thankfully, Lou's keys were on the floor inside the front door, as expected.

The flat was packed with inebriated and impoverished antipodean artists. After introductions, Lou put on some toast.

'Has anyone seen the apricot jam?' she asked, having looked in the fridge and cupboards.

'Oh, that was delicious,' said the old lady on the sofa.

'Thanks. Do you know where it is?'

'I think it's all gone,' she said.

Lou went hot. She needed to cry. But there was nowhere to go. The flat was overflowing with arseholes. Someone had moved into Becks's room. ('Hope you don't mind, she's been paying sixty quid a night for a flat-share in East Kilbride. Do you know where that is? Do you know anything about how terrible things are in East Kilbride?') Another, twenty-one-year-old Giuseppe, had taken ownership of the second sofa in the living room and was already officially best friends with the old lady on the other one. He was even taking care of her medication because the time difference really *was* confusing. In Lou's room, a guy called Barry was sleeping on a camping mat between the two single beds.

'Hope you don't mind,' Becks said.

Lou minded so much. She wanted to yell at everyone about the jam, her mum's jam. She wanted to scream about money. She should be compensated or at least consulted. She wanted to step on Barry's snoring face, but the new Lou didn't step on people's faces. She was way too happy to do that.

Instead, she tucked herself into bed and sobbed as quietly as she could, until Cam tapped her on the shoulder.

'They were demolishing it,' he said, holding up her mum's jar, which still had two inches of jam in it. 'Hide it from the fuckers.' He nestled the jar into her duvet and went to bed.

On Day Three she told Tim more about her new job. She was nervous about starting. What if the men were really scary? Did he know what MAPPA meant? Could she be in danger?

'Shouldn't you have asked these questions before now?' Tim said. 'Seriously, it sounds like the worst job in history. I don't think you should do it. It doesn't sound safe at all. What security systems do they have? How are you supposed to defend yourself in there? Alone – you? – having a pyjama party with five of Scotland's most dangerous criminals?'

'But it's three night shifts a week,' Lou said, 'four days off. I can go to Paris. I can nip across to Rome. They've done their time, they won't scare me. And you're right, there are only five residents.' Lou had been to Alan's hostel in North Melbourne (he shagged her in the office). There were ninety guys in there. The night workers always looked bored, they were always watching telly. 'Five guys,' she said, 'with amazing stories to tell, I bet; and it's in a beautiful old house in the centre of a gothic Disneyland; just up the road from my stunning Georgian apartment.' There, she had almost persuaded herself.

'Come,' said Tim, 'let's decide on the machines.'

'Machines?'

'Fruit machines, online. Fiver maximum. If we win more than ten pounds, we stop betting, and you keep the job. If we lose all our money, you find a better job. It won't be hard. All the cafés and bars are short of staff.' Tim found a bench outside a pub, got out his phone, settled himself there for the serious business of making a five-pound bet. 'Ready?' he said, patting the seat beside him.

'No, that is not a deal,' Lou said, still standing. She wasn't into gambling. She didn't understand it. It seemed like a huge waste of time when you could just throw your money away. Also, she didn't want to get a job in a café.

Too late, he had cracked his knuckles, said some magic words—

'Here we go, here we go.'

His phone was making the sounds of Las Vegas. He had placed a five-pound bet and…

'Damn,' he said.

'We lost?'

'We won – twenty pounds.' He showed her the balance on his screen. His grin was catching. 'Which means you have to go to your terrible job. Wanna check out a real casino?'

She did.

It was in a beautiful basement flat about a ten-minute walk from the centre of town. Tim was more than welcome in this exclusive private club. He changed his twenty pounds into a chip, as well as three other twenties, ordered two French martinis at the bar, took a seat at the roulette table and started placing his chips.

It was all very quick after that. She stood behind him (because he asked if she would). He cracked his knuckles – 'here we go, here we go' – and spun the wheel. Before she knew it he had won fifty quid. She took over after that, first with his fifty, which she lost in two seconds, and then with her own money. She won four hundred pounds if you didn't count the seven hundred she lost.

Despite losing, they were on a high and agreed they should get higher. Tim made a call, met a man in the toilets of a small, dark pub. They took cocaine on a tour bus, went round and round and round the town, waving at people, laughing too much, kissing too much.

'Stop that or I'll call the police,' someone said. 'You should be in jail, the pair of you.'

They'd been alone on the top deck for a while. Lou's bra was undone and a hefty American tourist was glaring at her and looking for a seat as far away as possible.

'Sorry,' Lou said, tidying herself up.

'We're a pair of sex offenders,' Tim whispered.

Lou giggled, then stopped. Eek.

In the early evening Tim took her into a graveyard and snapped photos of her hands gripping the top of an old granite headstone (*Andrew Mackintosh Laidlaw, 1817-1882*). They drank whisky in Rose Street, ate pies at the station, kissed goodbye. What a day. Lou could imagine spending every day with Tim.

CHAPTER SEVEN

Tim texted her the next morning: *Fancy a trip to the country? I need to pick some things up from my sister's place. We've sold the family home* ☹

Lou had pins and needles all over as she walked to the station. This had happened with Alan, in the early days. He would pick her up in his soft top, drive her along Melbourne's beaches, putting the roof down when they got further out than Brighton, and take her for a picnic, etcetera. She fell in love with Alan then, and she remembered how awful it was, like morning sickness but all the time. In the first fortnight, she lost two stone and her boobs. She must be falling in love with Tim. No, she couldn't be. After five days? Perhaps it was yesterday's martinis and cocaine. She upped her pace, she couldn't wait to see him. They were to meet on the platform. They were to travel by train together, like couples in olden times, holding hands, having a wholesome day out.

She'd never met a boyfriend's family before. Well, she met Haz's mum at the Coles check-out in Seymour. Lou always said hello. She always said hello. But for the first time ever, Lou was invited to the family home of a man/boy/boyfriend/she-had-no-idea-what-yet. She was to meet the sister, the niece, the nephew, the dog. She was, surely, to be introduced as the new girlfriend, greeted with a hug. 'Thank *god,'* her new sister-in-law would say. And, 'We are going to be the best of friends.'

This was, in fact, almost exactly how it went.

Except that she and Tim did it in the toilets on the train.

And Tim's sister didn't have a dog, or a second child. She had a son, Nathan, aged fourteen, who was waiting with his mother at the station.

'This is Lou, my girlfriend,' Tim said.

'Oh yeah?' said Lou. 'First I've heard of it.' She shook Nathan's hand and gave Tim's sister a hug. She seemed kind and comfortable, Ruth, if a little less lucky than her brother, genetically. Lou wasn't sure they'd be *best* friends.

The drive was so colourful that Lou needed sunglasses: gentle fields of brilliant greens. She could melt into this countryside, drive these little roads forever.

When they turned off the single track, and through the huge stone and iron gates at the front, she thought they had arrived. There was, after all, a lovely cottage to the right with green painted windows, slate roof, roses in the garden.

'That's the gatekeeper's house,' Tim said, and they continued up the tree-lined drive. After about four hundred metres, Lou arrived at a Scottish cliché – a stone lion was spurting water in the middle of the circular drive, there were sweeping stairs leading up to a *Rocky Horror* door. It was a castle. There were even turrets up high with scary windows.

'Welcome to Tavisdale Lodge,' Ruth said, parking the car behind a large removal van.

'Should I call you Lord Timothy? Or would you prefer Mr Darcy?' Lou whispered to Tim.

'This is hardly Pemberley,' he said. 'It's a hunting lodge. It looks bigger than it is. Anyway, it's not going to be ours anymore.'

'It must be so hard to leave this place,' Lou said as her new sister-in-law unlocked the crazy door with her crazy key.

'It's too much for me and Nathe,' she said. 'Freezing in winter.'

'What a place though,' Lou said. There was a maze in the garden, a pond, pretty paths. Lou was moving herself in.

'Time's right for us to sell and divvy up,' Ruth said, smiling at her brother. 'Come on in, I've made pancakes.'

Don't think about boating, don't bring up boating, no boating, Lou thought as she followed the others into the hall. There was a central staircase. The bottom half of the walls were lined with dark wood, the top decorated with the heads of dead animals, including a large fish, which may well have been caught in a boat.

No boating.

There was also a large wooden cabinet on the wall, empty now, once for guns, she supposed. This was a hunting lodge after all.

Young Nathan, sullen and awkward, headed upstairs – to

his wing, she imagined. There were dust marks on the walls where artwork had been taken down. From what she could see, most of the furniture was gone. The only picture on the wall was a family portrait crammed between two dead stag heads. Tim, at around ten, was beside Ruth, about twelve, their glamorous parents standing behind them on the front steps of Tavisdale Lodge. They all looked pretty miserable.

'Cute,' Lou said.

'You're not taking that one?' Tim asked his sister, a little pale as he looked at the painted faces of his dead parents.

'I can't bring myself to take it down,' Ruth said, leading the way to the enormous country kitchen at the back of the mansion. 'Do you want it?'

'No, you're right. It belongs here,' Tim said.

She was a little bit strange, this Ruth. She only had small talk, but wasn't good at it. 'So you're from Melbourne?' She had no interest in listening to the answer. She was busy, right enough, laying out a five-star breakfast on the dining room table adjacent to the kitchen: fresh fruit, pancakes, bacon and maple syrup, croissants.

Ruth and Tim took their time making coffee in the kitchen. They were whispering, a little heatedly, then turning on the milk frother and talking more loudly. Lou still managed to get a few words.

'I am not doing this again,' said Ruth. 'I am not going through this again.'

Ruth turned the machine off, took some notes out of her wallet and gave them to Tim. The pair came back in with scowls on their faces. There was tension at the table.

'Sorry about that,' Ruth said. 'Cash-flow issues. Be good to get this house sold.' She wouldn't look at Tim, she was mad about something. They chewed slowly, no chatter, just looked out at the garden.

After what seemed like an hour, Lou wanted a drink. She was not used to silence, or dining sober, or being with Tim sober. She'd rather her father was yelling about the strawberries being rotten and that her mother was relaying every little thing that happened in her ever-colourful and sociable day. It made her smile, thinking of her father yelling. He always felt bad about it afterwards and tried to make amends in some small way – helping with homework, taking them out to get ice-creams and lollies. This quiet vibe was messing with her head. 'Is it hot in here?' she asked, fanning her face.

Ruth opened the windows and the door. It helped.

'To think you've eaten in this dining room together since you were little,' Lou said. She couldn't count the number of kitchens she'd eaten in with her family, Dad at one end, Mum opposite little Lou, all of them using their forks properly, eating their soup the right way, finishing everything on their plates, always chatting, sometimes yelling, but never with their mouths open.

'We have, on and off, it's true,' Tim said. 'I can't

remember a time when this table wasn't here.' He took his sister's hand because it was trembling.

'It is hard to leave,' Ruth said, no longer angry. 'Now, one more coffee then I need my worker bees.'

Excellent. Lou loved being a worker bee. Anything would be easier than sitting at a table in silence.

❁

The drawing room was filled with hundreds of knick-knacks that ranged from two centimetres tall (gold cat figurine) to two feet tall (plaster bust of some guy). She supposed this was art and marvelled at the luck of this clan, who travelled the world's souks to find the perfect little gold cat. In the corner there was a table with flat boxes, bubble wrap, pens and labels. Lou was in heaven.

Tim put country music on and sang as badly as she did. At one point, during a Dolly number, he grabbed her by the waist and they did a twirl. They wrapped and packed and laughed and occasionally kissed. She liked Tim sober, didn't mind herself either.

When they finished Lou did a 'sweep' of the room. She was very good at this. She found a tiny silver egg behind a curtain and a small wooden box at the back of a high shelf. The box was about ten inches by five, with two fancy medals and some old coins inside. One of the medals was gold and star-shaped, with a ribbon that looked like a school tie. 'What's this?' she said, holding up the star coin.

'That's ... show me.' Tim took the box, looked at the contents sadly, then closed the lid. 'Wow, Dad used to collect coins and stuff. World War Two, this one, Air Crew Europe Star. Thanks.'

'That's for the auction house.' Ruth was at the door. 'I was wondering where it got to.' She walked over to Tim, took the box, and smiled. 'Wow, you guys are a pretty fine team,' she said. 'Great job, thank you.'

'Want to go for a swim?' Tim said.

Ruth wasn't keen. Nathan was gaming upstairs.

It was just the two of them, walking through the rose garden, the maze, the vegetable patch, the field, down to the pond. They chickened out of a swim and dangled their feet from the jetty instead. 'So, the girlfriend thing,' Lou said.

'You don't want that?'

'I've known you five days. Of course we're not boyfriend/girlfriend. You really should have talked to me first.'

Tim, still sitting, skimmed a stone. Two bounces.

'But I like it,' Lou said, standing and taking position to skim her stone. Three, no four, bounces. 'I don't want it to stop.'

'I'm too intense, sorry,' he said, standing and taking her hand. 'We'd better go, hey?'

'Or you'll turn into a pumpkin,' Lou said.

'Something like that,' he said.

Tim only took one item from the house: a green tin, shoebox size, with a little padlock.

'What's in the box?' Lou asked.

'Nothing much,' he said. 'I'll tell you another time.'

Before leaving for the train, Lou took a photo of the siblings on the front steps. They were both crying in it. Afterwards, they hugged. Young Nathan came outside and joined them, nestling into his mother's chest, taking the hand of his Uncle Tim.

Lou did not want to rush them, but Becks was getting needy.

Where are you? she'd texted hours earlier.

I've hardly seen you. Can I cook you an early dinner in the flat tonight, to wish you luck for tomorrow?

I'm gonna assume you're on, she texted later.

See you at six, she texted again.

I'll be there, Lou replied on the train. She and Tim were holding hands, too sleepy to have sex in the toilets.

There were ten other Australians at the dinner table. They'd all just returned from flyering; pitching their gigs at drunk passers-by, using the full force of their confrontational personalities. The floor was littered with piles of glossy A5

pieces of paper, all with stupid things written on them. (*The Year I Pulled My Tongue Out; Bipolar in the Basement: Fuck Toads.*) These poor performers had a two-hour window between flyering and gigs. At least two of them were method actors who stared ahead, seemingly unable to hear or see anything. They must have been playing dead people.

'To Grandmum and Grandad,' Becks said, 'for our visas. And to the Mad Kangaroo and her exciting new job.'

'And to Becks,' the New Zealand rock-opera singer said, 'who writes only because she has a voice within her that will not be still.'

They all clinked their fizz while Cam served the curries and condiments he'd made. At first Lou wished she was anywhere else, but she changed her mind after the lamb bhuna. As she ate and drank, she asked questions and found herself interested in one or two of the answers. She promised to go to all of the gigs. They all sounded so amazing, why wouldn't she go? She was also very interested in joining a pilgrimage to Plath's grave in Hebden.

The dessert, made by Becks, was pavlova with cream and crushed Cadbury's Flakes and strawberries. Lou had two pieces and made two promises to her cousin: she would go to her play tomorrow before work. And she would make more time for her. 'I might go for morning walks after my nightshifts,' Lou said, 'make sure I do something with the day. Want to come?'

Becks said she'd love to, then left, along with everyone else in the flat. Lou was alone at last. She opened windows, cleared the table, did the dishes, scrubbed the bathroom, cleaned the toilet, vacuumed the carpets, washed the floors, straightened throws and cushions and sofas, folded bedding, shut windows, left a note on Becks's pillow: *Love living with you!* She went to bed happy.

A huge crowd arrived back around 3am, voices loud, bottles clanking. They turned the music on in the lounge and began dancing to songs Lou didn't recognise. Cam came in when the dancing began, went to sleep straight away. She should get the same earphones as him. At around seven in the morning, two or three people were still singing. Lou tossed and turned till mid-morning, then gave up trying to sleep and started cleaning around the unconscious bodies in the communal area. She filled five bags with bottles and rubbish. She did the dishes, swept, put coats on hooks, straightened rugs, dusted skirting boards, put mugs at the same angle in cupboards, created a shoe area in the hall, placed them neatly in a line, started cleaning windows.

'What the fuck,' young Giuseppe said. 'I'm trying to sleep.'

'Any chance you can close the curtains?' said the old lady on the other sofa.

They rolled their eyes at each other. Like *she* was the weird one. They probably talked about Lou behind her back, said all sorts of mean things, like her housemates in St Kilda did, and like all her best friends ended up doing when her move date approached. *Why bother with someone who's leaving?* they seemed to say, removing her from party-invitation lists and netball teams. Before swearing at the poor performers about getting the fuck out of her house, something Aussie Lou might well have done, she rushed to her bed and hugged her pillow.

When she woke it was 7pm. The flat was empty. There was a note from Becks on the kitchen bench: *Thank you for cleaning! I love living with you so much MORE!*

7pm? Her first shift started in two hours.

And she had missed Becks's play.

CHAPTER EIGHT

Lou pressed the buzzer at nine on the dot, then knocked on the door because the buzzer didn't work.

'I'm Big Neil,' five-foot-five Neil said, shaking her hand and then warning her in the hall: 'Polly was on today so don't expect any kind of handover.'

Neil showed her into the front room, which was probably the living room in all the other terraced houses in the street. In this one, it was the office. The hot, thick, smelly air hit her throat, made her cough a little. There were two wobbly, scratched desks, both in stupid places, two sofas (ditto), five semi-broken office chairs and a nest of ugly coffee tables. There were notices on the walls – *Housing Benefit*; *Bowel Screening*; *IN/OUT*; *Fire Regulations* – but not enough to cover wallpaper rips and Blu-tack stains. Spiky Polly was sitting on one of the sofas having a whispery conversation with a dark-haired, overweight woman in her thirties. Neil seemed nervous about interrupting them; he decided not to. Lou wondered who the woman on the sofa was – a visitor, a colleague, a friend? She must be important for them to have to wait like this, seen not heard, servants at the door. Whoever she was, she seemed to have a lot to whisper about.

If there were ever original features in this house, they

were long gone. Oak floors had turned to green carpet tiles, ceiling roses were now strip lights and the doors were flat, heavy and fireproof. If not for the ceiling height, she could have been in a portacabin in Puckapunyal. If not for the view, too. Outside was a world of turrets and tunnels, of stone houses that didn't exist down under. Lou spotted a neighbour in the front garden opposite. Preppy, pastel and not impressed. He shot her some disdain, picked up his ginger cat and shut the door. She could imagine how gorgeous his front room was.

'Lou's here,' Neil finally managed to say to Polly. 'I'm just gonna finish those forms with Rob and double-check everyone's in for the night.'

Polly didn't seem to care that the new worker had arrived. She didn't even stand up. 'Stacey, this is Lou,' she said, 'our new night worker.'

'Hi Stacey.' Lou put her hand out for a shake, but apparently this was the wrong thing to do.

'Stacey is Rob's wife. He's leaving us, moving back home in a few days. They're very excited,' Polly said.

Lou wasn't sure what to say. She'd hate to have to move back in with Stacey.

Stacey stared at Lou, bemused, then said: 'Does your mother love you?'

There was an image in her head, of a woman waving in a queue, clutching a jar of jam. 'Of course,' Lou said.

This caused Polly to straighten her back and tighten her little lips. 'You know, Lou, not everyone's mother loves them. You should never assume.'

'Oh,' Lou said, relieved that these two women would soon leave.

It wasn't soon, though. They sat there for an hour saying things that Lou did not understand. They both had aggro accents, nothing like the Billy Connolly one she was expecting, which Gregor and Big Neil complied with. Nothing like Linlithgow Timothy either – he said he got his English accent at boarding school. These two said 'ken' at the end of every sentence as if they had given each other the same puppy-love nickname. Lou worked out after a while that it must mean something like 'y'know'. Every word they said sounded menacing as well as depressing. She was thankful when Neil walked back in with a fat, moustached, blond man.

'This is Rob, Stacey's husband,' he said.

'Rob this is...'

'...your new night worker.' Stacey finished the sentence, turned it into something gross and threatening.

'Ah baby, give us a hug.' Rob bent over to reassure his wife that he would not fall for the pretty young night worker, his jeans lowering to reveal a dark, cavernous fifty-cent slot.

Stacey and Polly were gathering their things to go –

phew. 'She's parked at my house,' Polly said to Rob. 'I'll see she gets off safely.'

After waving his wife and Polly off, Rob headed to the basement for 'movie night'. At last, Lou had some time alone with her new BFF. 'Is that normal, for a resident's wife to be pals with the boss?' she asked Neil.

'No. Never tell them where you live. Never tell them anything. You tell them something personal, it'll seem like nothing, for example that you adore the linguine at Rico's, next thing you turn on the news and Rico's has been robbed.'

'How would you adoring Rico's linguine lead to a robbery?'

'It's a long story,' said Neil. 'Just remember that things can get out of hand here and you have to remember your boundaries. Golden rule, number one: tell the fuckers nothing, nada, nish.'

'Nish?'

'Tell them nothing. Polly is not normal. Don't let her seem normal. In fact, just a sec…' Neil pressed zero on his phone and spoke into it: 'Wednesday continued, 2130: Polly did no handover or induction with new night worker. Before she left just now she said: "She's parked at my house, I'll see her off." This was regarding Rob's wife, Stacey. She continues to have no boundaries with residents and to make toxic partnerships to the detriment of staff.'

He stopped recording and smiled. 'How about a tour?'

To the side of the office was a small room with a single bed in it.

'We used to do sleepovers back in the day,' Neil said. 'All waking shifts now. This bed remains here as one of many torture devices. You'll understand at around 3am. Also it's a test – see up there?' There was a camera in the corner, its light flashing. 'This is the only one Polly ever checks. She caught Jacky sleeping twice.'

'Poor Jacky.' She had no idea who Jacky was. 'Was she sacked?'

'You have to kill someone to get sacked. Even then you'd probably just get moved to a nicer job. No, Polly just likes to have collateral.'

'Is that why you're recording notes about Polly? So you have something on her?'

'I'm trying to get rid of her,' Neil said. 'It's best you're aware. She's evil. Since I started she's had at least three disciplinary hearings, dozens of formal complaints, nothing that sticks, she always talks her way round. But middle management want her gone. They advised me to make a note of everything.'

Lou took mental notes as Neil showed her the inefficient workings of the office, which she was already dying to reorganise.

'We call this Raymond,' he said, opening a small

backpack. 'He has everything you need to get by – master key, opens every room; work mobile, emergency numbers all programmed in; naloxone revival kit, you just gotta grab the syringe and go for it, just stab them, bang. You seen *Pulp Fiction*?'

'No.'

'That's good, don't do it like that. Stab them in the thigh or the arm muscle. I'll show you later. There is also this special knife, see? It's for cutting nooses.'

'You're joking.'

'You've got to keep Raymond on your person all night,' he said, putting it on his back. 'Never let him out of your sight. They're always up to something. They have way more fun than us. Way more fun. Their parties are wild – always wind up with someone hanging on a clothesline with a firework up his arse or locked in a freezer at the Co-op. What I'd do to be a fly on the wall during the crimes this lot commit, showing their true selves, making their best worst decisions, then you'd see who they really are. No-one'd believe what they actually get up to. They'd have to tone it down for the drama adaptation. They know how to have fun is the truth of it, and I am jealous. Craziest my Saturdays get is three vodka martinis and half a blow job.'

'Half?'

'It's a long story.'

Neil got serious showing her the cameras on the office

computer, and how to enable and disable the alarm systems, when the landline rang.

'All good, Neens?' Neil scowled then raised his eyebrows as he listened to whatever drama was being conveyed by whoever Neens was. 'So she's in the cells till Monday?' He listened again. 'And the python's definitely still in her room. No, don't open the door, call the SSPCA. I'm here all night with the new worker – call if you need us. No, she finally left, with her chum Stacey. I know, I know. Let's grab a drink soon eh … Better go, I've got myself a shadow called Lou. Say hi to Neens, Lou,' he said, holding the phone up.

'Hi, Neens.'

Phone back at his ear, Neil said: 'Lovely. Too lovely for this place.'

Yay, Lou was managing to come over as lovely.

'Don't worry, I won't scare her with too much info. Ciao, my darling. Ciao ciao.' He hung up. 'Neens is on shift at the women's unit, five blocks that way. She's fabulous, you'll love her.'

Neil's tour continued to the sad square kitchen at the back of the house, with its sticky rectangular table and eight plastic chairs. 'We're having a leaving party for Rob. We could start decorating later if it's quiet.'

It'd need a ten-hour scrub first. And better systems in the fridge and freezer: food bags, labels. She'd find small baskets for the pantry. She'd need scourers and Fairy Liquid and bleach and bicarb and a tablecloth and perhaps some special paint to decorate the yellowing roller blinds. She'd ask Neil later. What fun.

The basement was divided into two large entertainment areas. The back room had a table-tennis table and a dartboard (Velcro), a bookshelf filled with scabby-looking boardgames, and heaps of junk, like empty jars and old wrappers and lidless plasticware. The front room was the TV/Cinema room. *The Notebook* was playing on the huge screen. Rob was sitting in one of the armchairs at the front. A forty-something legless man dressed in shorts and an England football jersey had parked his wheelchair in the middle of the room. Engrossed in the onscreen melodrama, he kept wriggling his upper legs so that his ample stump skin flapped up and down, slapping against his thighs. To be nauseated by the knee-flap skin of a disabled man would not be very social worky, or even very nice, but it sounded wet.

Thankfully Neil was too gripped by the final care-home scene to notice.

'Who's that?' Lou whispered.

'That's Chuggy.'

'Why's he doing that with his legs? Does he have Tourette's?'

'No,' Neil said.

'Is it to stop bad thoughts?' Chuggy must have an awful lot of them.

'Don't think so,' Neil said. 'For him it's probably just like wriggling his toes, tapping his feet, poor thing.'

Neil was a better person than Lou. Stump foreskin didn't make him gag, even though Chuggy was going very fast now, getting faster, faster. It was a sexual noise, that's what it was, and he knew it, and he was loving it. Of course. Skin slapping against skin. Chuggy was practically having a full-on wank right there in front of everyone.

'Shall we?' Neil said, the elderly couple on screen now dead.

Lou followed Neil up to the ground floor. 'Why is Chuggy here? Is he a sex offender?'

Before answering, Neil took her into the office and shut the door. 'Sorry, sound travels in the hall, so always shut the door, it's like a vault in here. No, he's not a sex offender. He's Chuggy Chatroom.'

Neil's dramatic pause was a lot of pressure. 'Chuggy Chatroom?'

'You haven't heard of him? No, really? Chuggy Chatroom?'

She didn't want to admit how little she knew. 'Is there a case file I can read?'

'There's a referral form on the system,' Neil said, 'and handover notes, worksheets. Polly refuses to use computers. She keeps paperwork somewhere, even though we're not supposed to. Has her own secret filing cabinet, and boxes of stuff the guys don't want kept in their rooms. She tells us bugger all, says we should only know what we need to know. Use Google, it's more detailed and more up to date than our system anyway. You can find all of our guys online – podcasts, documentaries, even drama adaptations. You'll know Lunchbox of course.'

One day maybe she would know something, even one thing would be great.

'Lunchbox. Da da da da da da da da da da daddle da da da da…' Neil had dance movements to go with the tune, whatever it was. 'Oh my god – you don't know Lunchbox. Scotland's answer to Jimmy Savile?'

She didn't have a clue who Jimmy Savile was either.

'Our very own Gary Glitter?'

That rang a bell, not a loud one.

'The Caledonian Rolf Harris?'

Ah. That kind of bad boy.

'No-one can know Lunchbox is here,' said Neil. 'He is the most despised man in the country, folk hate him. Don't tell a soul, not even your best friend. The papers and the podcasters and the victims and their vigilantes are always trying to find him. We had someone crawl into the roof space in the winter, tried to get in through the manhole. Another pretending to be his nephew. He's had to move seven times since he got out. They're always knocking on the door, looking all innocent and talking all nice. They might message you, phone you. "Hey Lou, do you want to make a quick two K?"'

She really did fancy making a quick two K. She'd gone through so much cash since she arrived.

'You could be at a bar and someone way better-looking than you might ask if you want a drink. You're a seven, he's a ten. I'm talking about me, the seven, you're probably a good 9.5, but two points are just for the tan, which will deduct several points when you get older. But listen, if he seems too good to be true, says you have the most enticing smile and that he wants to rub his face in your chest hair, it'll be a journo.'

'Gotcha,' Lou said. Neil did tend to go on and on.

'Do not talk to the press about Lunchbox. You say "no comment". What do you say?'

'No comment.'

'You'll know Timmy the Kid at least.'

'Timmy the Kid…' She should stop pretending there was a chance she might have a fact buried somewhere in her head.

'Jesus Christ, you really are from the other side of the world. Let's do a quick room check then I'll fill you in.'

Neil liked to prepare a snack for the residents for the midnight room checks. Tonight it was raisin toast and hot chocolate with marshmallows on top. Lou was in charge of heating the milk and stirring the chocolate. Neil did the toast and the marshmallows.

'This makes it a pleasant visit rather than a draconian search,' he said.

'What are we checking for?'

'That they're in, that they're okay, that they have no weapons, no drugs, no alcohol, no tied-up women…'

She wanted to ask what she was supposed to do if she found a tied-up woman, but it sounded weak. Instead she asked: 'What's Rob's nickname?'

'Rob hasn't got a nickname. Or a true-crime documentary or even a podcast, wee soul. Just the *Dunfermline Courier* for him. He's just Rob the fucking prick. He's a flasher and frotter, mostly on trains, and there's also a sexual assault. He's done well. It's now eleven months and twenty days since he got out, and he hasn't flashed, frotted or sexually assaulted once. We're going to have a party.'

'Are you joking?'

'No. Do you bake? I'm thinking red velvet but if you have other ideas…'

He obviously did not want her ideas, which was lucky as she didn't want to make Rob a cake.

Neil put the tray of goodies on the electric stair lift and they followed it – very slowly – up to the first floor. Neil gave it to Lou to carry up a narrower staircase to the second floor. She wished he hadn't. She was never very good at balancing things.

'Hey, Rob, supper!' Neil said, knocking twice on the front room and going in.

Rob's room was beige, tidy and organised. There were forms laid out on his desk – one was medical, one had a parole header, she couldn't make out the others. He had already folded all the clothes he had (a sad pile of trackies and T-shirts and boxers with easy-access slits), which he planned to pack into the binbags Stacey had brought in for him. He was now tackling the large pharmacy in the corner: inbuilt shelves, lined floor to ceiling with pretty little shot-sized bottles. Not booze, he wouldn't be allowed that.

'He's a flavour buff,' Neil said. 'A vintage vaper, our Rob. Goes way back. He's got everything from tuna to haggis and neeps.'

Those flavours seemed very closely related, she thought, not a wide range at all.

Rob continued to wrap each of the two hundred or more bottles in brown paper, sticky-taping each carefully before laying it to temporary rest in the large plastic crate Stacey had brought for him. He had a lot to say about his collection, but Lou didn't listen or understand much – other than that he'd given up a month ago; the collection was probs worth a fortune; he'd kill for a tobacco-flavoured one; did she have a cigarette?

Rob's duvet was stained with something. Was it blood, at the bottom right? She wondered if she should say something. It was large and reddish brown. Maybe it was poo. Probably. Or a shadow, ah, it was a shadow. She was glad she hadn't said anything.

Two walls were filled with photos of children. His were the blond ones, probably, big-headed boys with unlucky features. The other two had Stacey's scowl and dress size already. His TV took up a third wall, must have cost him a fortune. She wondered why he bothered using the cinema room in the basement when he had all this.

Rob should read the room. Neil should read the room. She had been holding a tray of hot drinks for ages. They were talking about birthday-cake flavour and egg-fart super-clouds. Rob was still wrapping (olive and feta presently), SO slowly.

At last, Neil moved a wad of sticky tissues on Rob's pine bedside table. He took a mug and a plate from Lou's tray and placed them down. It was time to settle in for the night, perhaps with a nice movie.

Rob turned on his television: *Dahmer*, episode seven.

'Don't let him give you nightmares,' Neil said, glancing around the room, then exiting, satisfied.

There were still four full mugs on the tray. Lou's arms were getting sore.

'Seriously, you've gotta watch this one,' Neil said, knocking on room two, then letting himself in.

'Hiya,' said Neil. 'Lou this is—'

'Tim…' She had said this out loud. It was Timothy. 'Can you take the tray?' she managed to say.

Neil leapt in, got it just in time.

CHAPTER NINE

Her head was boiling, spinning. She rested her back against the wardrobe, determined not to faint. She always did the same thing, over and over again. Stupid, stupid girl. *'Y'know he roots Sharon Henderson, yeah, down by the creek?'* (Haz's mate's sister, Puckapunyal.) *'You know he's married yeah?'* (Mick, Melbourne.) *'You do realise he's a dangerous criminal?'* (No-one said this, Edinburgh.)

'We've met,' Tim said. 'Briefly, at *Plath! The Musical.*'

'You both went to *Plath! The Musical*?' Neil said.

'We did,' said Tim.

'What a coincidence,' said Lou.

'Small town,' said Neil. 'You'll get used to it. The advice is we should ignore each other when we meet outside – staff and residents, I mean. It can be awkward otherwise.'

Tim's room, which was on the top floor opposite Rob's, had been given a lick of paint (chalky blue, the same colour as the drawing room at Tavisdale Lodge). All the furniture was sturdy and expensive, like the polished antique wardrobe that had saved Lou from falling. She moved away from it, steadied her feet on the Victorian rug. The room was obviously filled with furnishings from Tavisdale. There was an ornate mirrored dressing table, a roll-top writer's desk, a shiny wooden sleigh bed covered with soft throws and pillows. Tim shut the lid of his laptop, swivelled his expensive office chair from side to side.

'Any gambling today?' Neil said.

'No.'

On the roll-top desk there were several books about maths and philosophy, a pack of cards and a framed photo of the family on the steps of Tavisdale. The tin box he'd taken from the family home was on the floor under the window. Three banjos rested on the mantlepiece above the closed-off fireplace.

Everything in the room rang true. This was the Tim she thought she knew, except for the whole MAPPA thing.

'Have you worked out how to repay your debt?' Neil said.

'What?' said Tim.

'The money you owe – how much is it again?' Neil was unafraid of embarrassing Tim in front of the new worker.

'It's just fifteen hundred. I asked my sister,' Tim said, 'like you suggested. She'll help me out till the house is sold.'

Okay, so he owed some money and he'd committed a crime. But it was probably only a nice, neat money crime; it probably didn't hurt anyone that mattered.

Unless he was a sex offender.

She had let this man pin her against a bin, fondle her on an open-top bus.

Holy shit, could he be a sex offender? She needed air.

The view out the window was of the back courtyards of the terraced houses, widening out to a view of her own street, just two blocks down the hill. That was her building in the distance, was it? She wondered if Tim could actually see her bedroom from here. That would be another big coincidence, wouldn't it, if he'd seen her vomit out the window that time?

'No alcohol today?' Neil asked.

'None.' His face reddened, might have been with shame.

'Cocaine, cannabis?'

'No, no, I've been good.'

'How was flat hunting?'

She didn't realise he was flat hunting. Buying or renting? she wondered.

'Good. There's one in Leith I like.'

Leith sounded nice.

'There is a faint whiff of weed in here,' said Neil.

'It's coming from outside,' said Tim.

Neil sniffed at Edinburgh's night air though the open window – 'Right enough' – then he closed it.

Lou put Tim's snack on his desk. The framed family photo on the shelf was a copy of the large portrait she'd seen at the family home. Tim and Ruth on the steps; proud and prosperous parents behind. She noticed some material draped over the back of the portrait, with the word 'woman' on it. You could only see one tiny corner from the front, so most people wouldn't know it was a pair of Wonder Woman underpants. She could see some of the name tag – the word 'Lou'. If she lifted the pants off the frame, she would see the second word – 'O'Dowd'.

'Ooh, this is good,' Tim said, sipping his sticky drink. He noticed that Lou had spotted the pants and he flicked them. They fell, hidden, behind the frame. 'Thanks so much, Lou. Thanks, Neil.'

She had to get out of this room, find somewhere private where she could fall to the ground and be unconscious. She made it to the top of the first floor and into the electronic chair at the top of the stairs. She put her head between her legs, breathed.

Neil followed her, placed the tray down beside her. 'Why are you freaking out? Is there anything I should know? Did you do more than chat with him? You didn't, did you?' Neil whispered.

'No, god, no, nothing.' She was already lying to her new best friend. Neil was going to be another one that would not be forever. 'I sat next to him at a matinee and fell asleep. Chatted for a bit in the foyer. I was just, I think my arms were just sore and I was a bit shocked. In the theatre he seemed so suave and successful. Here…'

'First good-looking resident since time began,' said Neil. 'But don't be fooled. He's a gambler. I'd rather be married to a heroin-user than a gambler. Total headfuckery.'

She wanted to say: 'What did he do?' It's all she could hear in her head: *What did he do? What did he do?* But noise travelled in that hall. This was not the time nor the place. Perhaps it would never be appropriate to ask. As per Polly, she should only know what she needed to know. Did she need to know what Tim did? *What did he do?!* 'It's all a little overwhelming,' she said. 'I'm a bit scared of everyone.'

'Excellent. I'd send you home if you weren't scared. Mostly you'll be bored out of your brain here, but you must always be ready for that special period each day of absolute terror. You've gotta be ready to pounce, no matter how asleep you've been. You've gotta be tough, no matter how creeped-out you are. Speaking of which,' Neil said, checking the time. 'C'mon girly girl, up, up. Come let me introduce you to Lunchbox.'

It was time to compartmentalise: to leave behind the Lou who'd given away her underwear at Waverley Station and lunched in silence at Tavisdale Lodge. Who was that, anyway, and what the fuck was she thinking? Her head was buzzing with questions that she must shut up – but she couldn't yet, because she'd been targeted, obviously, from the very beginning. By a serious criminal. *What could he have done?*

His crime was obviously serious enough to get more than four years in prison. Perhaps something not too ugly, though. Maybe the man he headbutted died – sad but not evil. He said it was the worst thing he'd ever done.

But she wasn't going to obsess about Tim. A five-day fling, that's all it was, and then it was over. She was now a night worker. She was surrounded by cool and crazy colleagues. She was dipping in and out of the chaos of criminality. She had a job to do, one that she actually liked (so far) and was going to get paid for. Employable Lou would not screw this up. Fuck Tim, whoever he was, whatever he wanted, whatever he'd done. She was already over him. She packed away the Tim she'd known, the one from Linlithgow, and taped him up nice and tight.

Lunchbox was on the first floor, in the back room. For some reason, Neil wouldn't knock on his door. 'Not yet, not yet,' he said, looking at this watch. 'Three, two, one, okay.' He knocked, went in. And there was Lunchbox, a tiny man in his eighties or even nineties, dressed in a short, floral silk kimono, standing on the bed, bare legs wobbling, rope in his hand, reaching to the ceiling.

'Hey, Lunchbox,' Neil said, ignoring the hook and the rope in his hand; ignoring the whole suicide situation, in fact. 'This is Lou, she'll be doing night shifts. Down you get.'

Lunchbox handed the rope and hook to Neil and sat down on the bed to cry. Neil put the mug and raisin toast on his bedside table.

One wall of the bedroom was lined with shelves filled with soft toys. At least five hundred of them, all squashed together. Another wall was covered with music awards and framed press cuttings and photos – in one, he was with Princess Diana. Once he was a rock god. Now he was the devil, sobbing.

'You didn't go out today?' Neil was looking at the dressing area, neat, untouched. There were two clothes racks in the corner with a wide range of suits and smart casual outfits. There was a hat rack hung with berets and bowlers and caps. Another hat rack was adorned with wigs. Sunglasses were laid out on the dressing table.

'You've not deleted your browsing history?' Neil asked.

'No,' Lunchbox said, his crying increasing in intensity as Neil checked his television and his phone.

'Great then, night night,' Neil said, putting the hook in his pocket and shutting the door.

'What the fuck?' Lou whispered in the hall.

'He's doing well actually, we've got him up to seventeen.'

'Seventeen?'

'He's into eleven/twelve-year-old girls. We've been helping him move up the way so when he leaves in two months he'll be law-abiding.'

'Law-abiding is seventeen?'

'Seventeen for him, on his licence.'

That was all too disgusting to digest. She would maybe try later. 'But the noose?'

'Does it every night at this time, on the dot, has done for ten months. For a while we did all the paperwork.'

'But what if he has another hook, what if we're late, what if he does it some other way?'

'He buys the same hook every day, piece of crap, none of it would work.'

'But what if it did?'

'Why stand in the way of progress?' Neil said, knocking on the door to the bedroom above the office.

This was room four, belonging to Chuggy Chatroom, who had managed to get from wheelchair to bed, and was snoring loudly. *Beaches* was playing on his laptop. Neil checked that he was playing a DVD and was not online. He turned it off, and tucked him in.

Maybe Tim was a classy thief, Lou thought, like a diamond-heist guy. She should not be thinking this way. She needed to tape that Tim box tighter.

Room five, next to Chuggy, was a twenty-something guy called Doug who hadn't been mentioned yet. Must be a boring one.

'Any tied-up women in the wardrobe?' Neil said, depositing snacks.

'No.' He was fidgeting in an uncomfortable dining chair, also watching *Dahmer*. If he had better clothes and surroundings he'd be a healthy seven. 'Oh, hang on,' Doug said, 'there's one over there, bottom drawer.'

Neil laughed, then spotted a baseball bat behind the door. 'What is this?'

'I've been telling you, I'm not safe.' Doug turned the television down, got serious. 'Sam and Tony followed me home tonight. I think they're waiting outside. They're going to break my legs.'

Neil handed Lou the tray. 'I'm gonna chat to Doug for a while. See you in the office?'

Her legs were shaking as she headed downstairs. Her arms too. Tim was leaking out of his box. The questions were getting louder. She was going to have to work out what to do, because, at the moment, she didn't have a clue.

She opened the door to the sleepover room and sat on the bed.

Timothy, she typed into her phone. Realising she didn't even know his last name, she got up and looked on the IN/OUT board. First names only. She checked the diary on the desk. Initials only. She tried the computer – she did not have the passwords yet. Back in the sleepover room, she sat on the bed and thought hard about what Neil had called him – that's right, she remembered, Timmy the Kid. She began typing: *Timmy the K—*

'You okay?'

She jumped. It was Tim, at the door. She stood up, the back of her legs against the sleepover bed.

'I didn't know who you were,' he said. 'I promise, I knew nothing till you told me about the job – our third date. Then all I could think about was telling you.'

'Move back,' she said.

Tim moved back into the office area, hands in the air. 'I didn't want it to end. I was too scared to tell you.'

'Bullshit.' Lou was in the office now. She took a seat at the desk, established the new dynamic.

'You came and sat next to me,' Tim said. 'You stalked me the following day, Please, Lou, please believe me.'

'You can see my bedroom from yours,' she said.

'No. Can I? Really?'

'If you have a telescope. Did you follow me into the close the other night?'

'No. I don't know where you live.' He sat in the chair on the other side of the desk.

She leaned in. 'You don't live in Linlithgow.'

'I live here, for another month.'

'And you don't move money from one side of the table to the other for a living.'

'I just throw it right off the table. I'm a gambler, that's my risk, my need, my brain disorder, my everything.'

'You saw me on Zoom with Polly, didn't you? My interview.'

'I did not.'

'"Morning!"' she mimicked his cheerful, thoughtful voice. '"I'll pop the kettle on."'

Tim sighed and fidgeted. Was that a tear? 'Maybe I saw your face, briefly. Okay, okay, I did. I'm sorry, but that's all.'

'I don't care about this job,' Lou said, 'just so you know. I'll find something else. It's a shit job with shit pay. So I suppose you knew about *Plath! The Musical* from my Instagram?'

'You are pretty open online – and in person, by the way.'

'You're admitting you did know who I was?'

'Yes, fuck it, I hate myself for it. I'm sorry. I knew who you were. You had a nice pad in Melbourne, looked pretty well off to me, and I fancied you like crazy, obviously. Plus, I just have to be honest, it's always useful to have someone on side here, you know, to not get fucking breached and sent back to B Hall for having a drink or missing the bus or placing one bet. Polly hates people like us.'

'Us?'

'She's into the Robs and the Dougs of this world. I'm on my own here and sometimes it's worse than prison. I'm really sorry, I'm an arsehole. For the first couple of days I didn't even feel bad that you always ended up paying.'

'Shut up,' Lou said. '"At first it was a bet then I fell in love…" I hate those movies. I don't think that girl should end up with that guy.'

'I will. I'll shut up,' he said. 'But I did try and talk you out of the job.'

'You placed a bet,' she said.

'I've never introduced anyone to Ruth, never. Ask her. She knows me, she knows this is different, how I feel about you. I promised her I'd tell you everything before we got there. She was angry I didn't. She likes you. She thinks you should run a mile.'

Lou needed to punch herself in the leg for listening to this shit. 'You can't blackmail me or revenge porn me. I look fabulous naked, I have no money, and I don't give a fuck about anything.' But it wasn't true. Revenge porn would totally work on her. She didn't want her mum and her dad and her Uncle Fred to see her shagging a criminal in an Edinburgh graveyard. And to her surprise, she did want this job. Within a couple of hours, her head was spinning with people and stories that she would never forget. And it came with time for a minibreak every week. She'd seen cheap flights to Dublin, she might head there Saturday. She would not let him take this from her.

'Can you forgive me?' he was saying.

And Lou was realising that he had managed a clever thing, diverting her with the details of their (not so) cute meet, when it was his crime that she needed to know about.

He tried to touch her hand.

She flinched, moved back. Thankfully there was a good distance between them when Neil came in.

'All good?' Neil said, baseball bat in hand.

'That Doug's?' Tim asked, pointing to the bat, then standing.

'I'm not at liberty to disclose.' Neil locked the bat in a metal cupboard.

'I'm worried about Doug.' Tim yawned. 'He's been really on edge, hope he's okay. Anyway, night night.' He seemed to take ages shutting the door behind him.

Lou was desperate. She had to know, but it would be pathetic, gratuitous. *(What did he do? Tell me what he did!)*

Neil sat opposite her at the desk, opened a packet of sweets and offered her one: 'Percy Pig?'

She took one, chewed. Damn, they were nice.

Neil smiled and offered her another one: 'He murdered his parents,' he said. 'Blew their heads off with a shotgun.'

CHAPTER TEN

This programme contains dramatisations of real events and violent content. Some names have been changed. Viewer discretion is advised.

PRESENTER: When a wealthy married couple is gunned down in their Scottish country kitchen…

Lou was now sitting on the toilet, volume as low as she could manage, watching a documentary on her phone called *Timmy the Kid from Tavisdale Lodge*.

999 Operator: 999 what's your emergency?
Timothy: Um, I've just come to check on my parents…
999 Operator: What's your name?
Timothy: I'm Timothy Wilson.

PRESENTER: The peaceful residents of the idyllic town of Tavisdale, Fife, are shocked and frightened and they are battening down the hatches.

Neighbour: I'm thinking is there a killer on the loose? Will he burgle my house next, will he kill me next?

PRESENTER: But no-one has anything bad to say about the Wilsons.

Employee: The Wilsons had status in Tavisdale, everyone looked up to them.

PRESENTER: Locals are even more complimentary about the only son, Timothy.

Professor of Business, University of St Andrews: He was a charismatic first year, very likeable. It was unfortunate that online gambling got a hold of him and derailed a promising academic career.

Stepsister, Ruth: Tim loved Mum and Dad. He'd never have done anything to hurt them. There was no reason for him to. They were still supporting him financially, he was still in the will, there was no big life-insurance policy. Precious objects, like his mother's sapphire-and-diamond engagement ring and our grandfather's war medal, were taken and never recovered. Tim didn't take that stuff. The police would have found it. It was a burglary. He was at home with me. He did not do this. And what I find hardest – what Tim and I both find the hardest of all – is that the person or people who murdered our parents got away with it. No-one except us is even looking for justice.

PRESENTER: Just seventeen years old, dapper Timothy is the one to discover his father and stepmother in a bloody mess on the slate tiles of their stunning country kitchen. And he's the one to call 999.

Timothy: I've been trying to get hold of them for ages. And the doors are locked and the key under the pot isn't there and I can't get in, but I can see something. I can see someone on the floor in the kitchen, like a leg.
999 Operator: What's your address there, Timothy?
Timothy: Oh my god, Dad. Oh god, oh god, that's Dad, there's blood.
999 Operator: Timothy, you're saying your father is on the floor in the kitchen and that you can see blood?
Timothy: Yes.
999 Operator: Is there anyone else in the house?
Timothy: My stepmum should be there too. I can't see her. I can't see anyone.
999 Operator: What's your address?
Timothy: It's Tavisdale Lodge, outside Tavisdale. Oh, the drawing-room window is smashed. I'm going to climb in.
999 Operator: Stay on the phone please, Timothy, there's help on the way.
Timothy: I will. Please, please hurry.
[Glass smashing.]

Timothy: Ouch. Dad? Dad!

[The phone goes dead.]

PING! Lou banged the toilet on the way back down. It was a text alert from Timothy:

Can we talk?

She muted her phone and returned to the office. Neil had positioned himself on a chair facing the front window, feet on the sill, a book (*Treating Addiction*) and a pack of Cheesy Wotsits on his lap.

'Come,' he said, 'pull one up beside me.'

His tablet was on the floor at his feet and was playing *I Should Be Dead*: the one where the dad and son crash their Cessna into the ocean and get attacked by sharks.

'I nearly got eaten by a shark once,' Lou said.

'No way.'

'I was swimming with Dad, in WA. And this shark came in really shallow and started circling me, then kinda jabbing me, picking a fight.'

'Oh my god…'

'Dad had already taught me what to do.'

'What?'

'Punch it in the nose, again, again, again, *poom, poom*, grab its snout if you can and direct it away or, if you've got a spear or a knife or something sharp, stab it between the eyes or anywhere in the head with all your might.'

Neil waited as long as he could before asking: 'Did you have to do any of those things?'

'I tried all three,' Lou said, eating another Wotsit. 'I felt bad about it afterwards, it wasn't a very big shark.'

'You were carrying a spear when you were swimming?'

'A knife,' Lou said, 'in case of sharks.'

The shark episode was now the bear episode: the one where the father and son go on a bonding trip, get lost, then mauled by a bear. That had never happened to Lou, not once.

'Camera's behind us, by the way.' Neil pointed to the flashing contraption in the back corner of the ceiling and stuffed some Wotsits in his mouth. 'Best bet is to sit here.'

Messages buzzed against her hip.

Eventually, the guy on the screen got away from the bear, but now he was falling down a cliff. Neil's binge eating was slowing. He was adding a pillow under his feet on the windowsill, adjusting another behind his head.

'How do we stay awake?' she asked. It was only 1am. Eight hours to go.

'It's easy. Just don't sleep.'

Neil started snoring almost immediately. She turned the volume up on the tablet, unsure which noise was more sackworthy. Maybe they'd balance each other out.

Tim had sent the same three messages to her phone, her Facebook and her Instagram accounts.

1. *I'm so sorry about what happened.*
2. *I just want to say thank you. This was the best week of my life. You are the most intriguing and beautiful and exciting person I have ever known.*
3. *I know it can't go on – it makes me so sad – and I will not mention it ever again. I move out in a month. We can do this. PS, I tossed the bag with your pants in a council bin a few blocks away. Sorry about that. I forgot they were on my desk.*

Delete all the photos please, Lou typed, expecting him to be asleep.

He replied two seconds later: *Already deleted.* … He was typing … *Don't forget to delete the ones on your phone too. I'm deleting all your contact details, all these messages. I won't be in touch on a personal level again. You have nothing to worry about. Bye*

Bye. No full stop. But she was supposed to be the one blocking him. *Bye*

Neil's head flopped forward and his snoring got louder.

She Googled 'Timmy the Kid' again, scanned the headlines:

'Twisted Motivations of Monster Son'

'Son Assassinates Parents To Pay Gambling Debt'

'Prodigal Son Shoots Parents'

'Parenticide at Tavisdale Lodge'

She didn't want to read any more about that now, it was scaring her. The house was silent apart from the buzzing of absolutely everything electrical. She wondered if there was a spare lamp in the building somewhere; if she could turn off that dreadful strip light. This was going to be a very long shift. She grabbed a pad and pen and began scribbling:

Start flat hunting

Jumper/s

Gym

Send message to Mum and Dad

She should just do that one.

Hi Mum and Dad, she typed. *Loving Edinburgh. Airbnb is gorgeous, Becks is so much fun. The job is really handy. Hope you're both well, Lou x.* She waited a few seconds and was about to switch off her phone when a message came in:

Oh, my darling, it's so lovely to hear from you. I've worked out how to see your Instagram posts. You are looking more beautiful than ever. We could not be prouder of you, with your job over there. Uncle Fred says Becks is loving it, spending time with you. Let's talk soon, in the evening, after Dad's work – he is missing you. So am I! Mum xx

The message brought on a wave of sadness, worse than the grief she felt when they buried Grandma O'Dowd in her favourite dungarees. Lou often had these tsunamis of homesickness in Brisbane and Sydney, but never for long. Her mum would listen to her – on phone or laptop – for hours, send her money or flowers. Her dad would drive all the way from wherever with food and firewood and tools and a list of ways to improve the situation.

How she had missed her parents in the Alan years. How she missed them now.

Another episode of *I Should Be Dead* was on – the one where a guy and his brother are on a bonding trip and one gets stuck in quicksand.

On her notepad, Lou drew a map of the rooms in the house. At the top there was Rob the flasher and frotter and sexual assaulter. (He was married to Stacey.) At the back was Timothy Wilson the double murderer and excellent shag. (*Double Murderer*, Lou wrote, underlined, must not forget.)

On the first floor there was the elderly suicidal rockstar, Lunchbox. And also Doug the paranoid drug dealer. And someone else. Who was it again, ah, Chuggy Chatroom.

'OMG, now he's being eaten by piranha?' Neil had woken – although he wasn't admitting anything.

'Why's he called Chuggy Chatroom?' Lou asked.

'He had an online chatroom for the suicidal. Encouraged two people to do it, livestreamed it, shared the movies around. FYI he's not an alcoholic, he hangs out at AA and other places where people are sad, like funerals and improv gigs. His behaviour's escalating, I reckon, he's reaching out for more and more victims. Really gotta watch he doesn't get into the dark web again – check all his devices thoroughly, every night. And whatever you do, do not ask him how he is. He's never good. He's always sad because it's Meredith's birthday, she would have been ninety-nine, or James's anniversary, he would have been a hundred and seven, or because today is the day, four years ago, that he was taken to prison. He will want to give you all the details. Just say "morning", "evening", never "how are you?"' Neil yawned, shuffled his head pillow.

'And why does he have no legs?'

'Diabetes.'

'Isn't that a bad idea, to have Chuggy who persuades people to commit suicide in the bedroom next to Lunchbox who's suicidal? … Neil?'

He was snoring again. She closed her eyes and tried to do the same but it was no use. Maybe because she was jetlagged. She was wide awake and her double-murderer boyfriend was sleeping upstairs and he wasn't even the scariest man in the house. In fact, the more she read online, the less scary he seemed, maybe even a little less guilty too.

LAST APPEAL LOST EVEN THOUGH GUN NEVER FOUND

DNA evidence meaningless says Timmy the Kid

'I lived there every holiday. I went through the window and followed the killer's path. You can hear this on the call, so of course my DNA is all over the place.'

Ruth Wilson continues to fight for her little brother: 'He has never hurt a fly,' she says. 'He is the most loving, generous person I know. He adored Mum and Dad. We both miss them so much and we want the person who killed them to be found and punished. We want justice. I will not stop until we find the murderers, until my beautiful caring brother is pardoned.'

It was 3am. The piranha had stopped feasting but hypothermia and dehydration were setting in. Lou decided to clean the kitchen.

On the way, she stopped and listened in the hallway. The house was quiet except for the humming electrics and maybe someone's television upstairs. She turned on the kitchen lights then – blinded – turned them off again. She found a bedside lamp in the sleepover room and put it on the kitchen bench, opening cupboards to find what she needed: gloves, cloths, spray, cream cleaner.

The cloths were old and stinky. She threw them out and cut up a decrepit floral tea towel, rinsing it thoroughly under hot soapy water. She wiped the cupboards one by one, putting chipped crockery in a box to be taken to the bin later. She was washing the unbroken mugs and saucers when she heard a bang out in the back courtyard. She looked out the kitchen window. There were two large men behind the bins. No, hang on, they might have been bins as well. No, hang on, one of them was moving – away, thankfully, disappearing into the darkness of the back lane. She was startled when Tim came in.

'Sorry,' he said. He was wearing a tiny dressing gown. 'Can't sleep, need a cuppa.' He began looking through the cupboards Lou had just cleaned. 'Have you seen the cups that were in here?'

'Here you go,' Lou said, handing him one of the sparkling-clean ones she had just dried.

'Actually, it's a particular cup, it's a tad decrepit,' he said.

'All the chipped ones are in that box. Was it the one with the boobs?'

'No.'

'World's Best Uncle?'

'It's the one with Spiderman on it. I'm embarrassed, it's a comfort thing.'

'Ah,' she said, finding the chipped mug and handing it to him.

He turned on the kettle, put a teabag in his Spiderman mug.

Lou started cleaning inch-thick brown stuff off the microwave and tried not to look at Tim's legs.

He poured hot water into his cup: 'It doesn't have to be awkward between us,' he said.

'It does if you're naked.'

'Ha, sorry. This is all I've got … It was a Christmas present.'

'When you were seven?'

'Seventeen,' he said, squeezing his tea bag, 'from my mum and dad.'

She stopped scrubbing the microwave. 'How did you get parole, Tim,' she said, 'after, what, eleven years, if you're Mr Innocent? Don't you have to take responsibility for your offence?'

'I lied to the parole board, to get out, to be here.' He poured some milk into his mug. 'You must understand that.'

Must she? 'What did you tell the parole board exactly? What did you say happened?'

'I repeated the words they used when they found me guilty.'

'I don't know those words.'

'I snuck out of the gatehouse in the middle of the night, unbeknownst to Ruth. I had a gun, a mask, I broke in.'

'And?'

'Then Dad came downstairs with a gun, scared me and I shot him and then Mum.'

She was imagining what Tim's eyes might have looked like through the holes of a black balaclava, and if his father recognised them. 'Did your stepmum come down with a gun too?' she said.

'The story's made up, Lou,' he said. 'It was the only way

to get out of prison. I was asleep at Ruth's. No-one scared me. No-one was shot by me.' He rinsed his teaspoon, put it in the drainer. 'Night,' he said, Spiderman mug in hand.

She melted a little as he walked off, with his birthday-boy dressing gown and his childhood mug. It was a good strategy, vulnerability, even if he had taken it a bit far. Still, aw, poor Tim. He was just a boy when he was locked up. He was still just a boy.

A bad boy. If she had to put a figure on it, she'd say there was a seventy-five-percent chance that he was a parent killer.

CHAPTER ELEVEN

By 9am Lou had cleaned, decluttered and rearranged all the rooms in the basement and on the ground floor. She had neatly placed twenty filled bin bags against the back wall of the games room and clearly labelled them so they could be checked by the other staff and residents:

Rubbish from Office
Rubbish from Kitchen
Rubbish from Games Room
Rubbish from Cinema Room
Lost Property, Broken
Charity Shop

Neil was finishing off notes on the computer when she came upstairs. 'Morning, my darling,' he said. 'By the way everything you need to know about everything is in this folder.' He unlocked the bottom drawer of the desk and pointed to a large folder. 'Key to this drawer is on the master set in Raymond.' He locked the drawer, put the keys back in the backpack. 'Has something changed?' He stretched his arms, looked around. 'You did some cleaning.'

'A bit,' she said, heading to answer the door. The next worker was a-knocking.

His name was Euan. He was tall and slender and ginger (head and beard).

'Nice outfit,' Lou said, surprised that he was dressed so well: tight-fitting designer suit pants, silky shirt, top button undone, casual linen jacket, suave, shiny shoes.

The handover with Euan consisted of Neil telling him that nothing had happened, bar the finding of a baseball bat in Doug's room. He had messaged Polly about this and she would deal with it on her late shift. There were several appointments in the diary for the day ahead: Lunchbox was having a Tinder date with a seventeen-year-old at seven (bowling), Doug had a review at court, Chuggy had an AA meeting at ten and then again at six. Hmm. Tim had a meeting with his parole officer at twelve and a drugs test at two.

Drugs test. What next?

Euan was happy to tell them all about himself even though it was 9.30am, thirty minutes after the end of shift, and even though she and Neil were both yawning. He'd had an interview at last, for his post-grad year with a defence firm, and he was going to hear back any minute. He had a good feeling about it. The guy who interviewed him was impressed by his work at SASOL; that he was immersing himself in the criminal world.

'Now I understand the outfit,' Lou said. 'Bit of lawyer power.'

'Euan here believes some of these guys are innocent,' said Neil.

'What about Tim?' Lou found herself saying.

'Tim,' said Euan, 'did not murder his parents. No way. Hundred percent. I would have got him off. All circumstantial.'

'Don't be delusional,' Neil said to Lou. 'Everyone in here is guilty, and prolific. None of them are good guys.'

'Telling ya,' Euan said. 'Tim's the victim of a great injustice. Doug's a goodun as well.'

'Doug!' Neil laughed. 'He's worse than the lot of them put together.'

'You're very judgy,' said Euan.

'Very,' said Neil.

Maybe he'd be her new BFF, this Euan, maybe they'd go shopping together.

She left the building at 9.45am, and – as instructed by Neil – bought a roll and square sausage with brown sauce at the Hill Café.

'You won't ever go back to link sausages,' he said.

She heard a car beep on the way out of the café. It was an Audi, parked across the road. It took a moment to recognise Tim's stepsister, Ruth, sitting in the driver's seat.

'Hey Lou, over here, it's me,' Ruth yelled through the open window.

Lou had just taken a mouthful of her new sausage

discovery and was desperate to take another five. She crossed the road and leaned down. 'Hi.'

'Hiya,' Ruth said. 'I wanted to catch you. Do you have a minute? I've come to apologise for my brother.'

Which part, Lou wondered, *the slaughtering or the lying?*

'He promised he was going to tell you before he arrived,' Ruth said. 'I'm sorry, I should have said something when he didn't. Yesterday was agony. Can I drive you home?'

'No thanks, I live just...' She almost pointed. 'I need the walk.'

'Have you got time for a coffee?'

They went back into the Hill, ordered cakes and lattes from a grumpy man, and took a rickety table in a cool and uncomfortable corner.

'If it's any consolation he does really like you,' Ruth said.

Lou's cake – a vanilla bomb – was a huge vol-au-vent-style pastry filled with custard and coated in thin toffee. It was too big to handle and too delicious not to. 'Oh my god,' Lou said.

'I know,' said Ruth, somehow managing to eat hers neatly. 'Remind me to get one for Tim on the way out. He loves these. I'm dropping off some washing and shopping for him too. Then Thompson Roddick, then home.'

'Thompson Roddick?'

'Auction house, for some valuable old junk. Tim could do with some cash. He blew his benefits the day he got paid again. Asking me for money all the time. Do you know if he's gambling? Has he been asking around for money, getting any loans or cards?'

'Um.'

'Does he owe any money to anyone?'

According to Neil, he owed at least fifteen hundred pounds. Lou realised, to her relief, that she wasn't allowed to pass any information on. 'It'd be breaching confidentiality if I did know anything,' Lou said.

'I'm not going to sugar-coat it,' Ruth said. 'It never ends. It scares me. How can I trust him when the house is sold? He'll blow it in a week. I know he will.'

Lou remembered Tim flashing those twenty-quid notes in the private casino. Sad and pathetic that it was probably his entire weekly income.

'He only ever takes a little bit from people,' Ruth said. 'Like his first and only girlfriend, Tanya. He stole six hundred pounds from her. He does try not to destroy anyone.'

'That's nice,' Lou said.

'I know, right. I'm hearing myself. It's amazing what you get used to. I never understood it till I went to Gambler's Anonymous with him in prison. At least with drug users you get a heads-up: you wake up and the laptop's gone. With a gambler you wake up and the house is gone and your husband no longer has terminal cancer.'

And your parents are dead? Lou thought. 'Would you tell me if you knew he was guilty?'

'I think I would. I can't even imagine it though. It's Tim. My wee brother. He's never been violent.'

'Didn't he headbutt someone once?'

'Oh yeah, he did, but the other guy hit him first, and last. Drunk fight, Tim lost. He makes spectacularly bad decisions but he doesn't kill people.'

'Is that really why you wanted to see me,' Lou said, 'to say sorry? Or is it to make sure I don't screw up Tim's parole?'

'If anyone screws that up, it'll be him,' she said. 'I know how you feel, Lou. He's lied to everyone he loves.'

Loves? 'I'm keeping it professional, so you know,' Lou said. 'Tim's parole is safe, don't worry.'

'I'll keep it that way too,' Ruth said, and as proof, she only paid for her own stuff, and she shook Lou's hand outside rather than giving her a sisterly hug.

On the way down the hill, Lou noticed that someone was walking a little too closely behind her. She stopped and turned to find herself face to face with Doug the paranoid drug dealer, minus his baseball bat. In the house he seemed relatively well kept and healthy. In the light of day, and with a lot of rich people in the street, he seemed sickly and tiny, much older than his twenty-five years. He looked like he'd been crying: glazed eyes, dark circles.

'I'm sorry,' he said. 'Did I scare you?'

She shook her head as if it was ridiculous – Doug, scary? – then felt bad about it because he probably wanted to be, a bit.

'I'm so sorry, I know you're off duty, but I have nowhere else to go. I really need your advice. Do you have two minutes? It's really, really important.'

Lou wondered what kind of advice she was supposed to give. If he asked her about benefits, housing, offending behaviour, she'd have to admit she knew nothing. Oh, hang on, she did have one piece of advice: 'Euan's in the building,' she said. 'He's a lawyer practically.'

'They were in the back lane last night. Did you see them?' he said.

'Who?'

'Sam and Tony … You didn't see anyone behind the bins?'

'No,' she lied without thinking, but now she had time to think about it she had made the right decision. She couldn't be sure who or what she'd seen behind the bins. And she had no idea what Sam and Tony looked like.

'Huge guys, no necks?'

Even if it was them, she didn't want to make Doug more

anxious. She stuck with her story. 'I didn't see anyone.' Mind you, she would no longer think of him as Doug the paranoid drug dealer, just Doug the drug dealer. Maybe one day he'd just be Doug.

'Before my sentence I owed their mum two grand,' he said. 'Biggest mistake of my life. Sam and Tony say she died of stress because of me, and that it's five grand now or they break my legs. They're such lovely guys, Sam and Tony, they were so kind to their mum. Great dads too, they both have wee boys. They don't want to break my legs, but I've driven them to it. I'm not safe here. I'm going to have to do something to get back inside.'

'Have you spoken to the police?' Lou said.

'I've gone to the station three times, and they're all "If you don't leave now we'll arrest you." And I'm: "That's why I'm here, that's what I want, that's what I'm asking for." And they're: "Go home, Doug, get some rest. Call your parole officer."'

'Have you spoken to your parole officer?'

'She said I should talk to my GP.'

'What did your GP say?'

'Police. Look, I won't ask for money.'

'That's good,' Lou said.

'I just want advice.'

'How about we chat tonight, yeah, see if we can make a plan? We can't talk here, it's not appropriate, Doug.'

'A plan, I'd like that. What time are you in?'

'Nine.'

'So we'll talk then. You'll help me?'

'We'll talk,' she said, feeling really rather good about herself. Someone needed her help, badly, and maybe she'd be able to give it – and get paid for it. 'But Euan is on shift now. Why don't you go talk to him? He's practically a lawyer. Go home and talk to Euan.'

'Okay, I will. Thanks, Lou,' he said, hovering on the pavement.

'You go first … back up the hill,' Lou said. 'Don't follow me again. If you do, I'll call the police.'

'Please do,' he said.

She waited till he was out of sight, turned the corner and walked ten feet to her front door, smiling all the way.

Lou had forgotten her promise to Becks – morning walks after nightshifts! What a stupid idea. What was she thinking? She wanted to sleep so badly.

'Ten minutes,' Becks said, knocking on her bedroom door.

Lou donned her sporty stuff, splashed her face with cold water and tried to match her cousin's pace, if not her enthusiasm.

'You have to tell your boss,' Becks said, swinging her unashamed power-walking arms.

They were nearing the top of Arthur's Seat and Lou was already regretting her open-and-honest policy with Becks. She'd told her everything.

'Or leave. Immediately. Honestly, really, Lou?'

Lou was panting. She needed to quit the social smoking. Or be a whole lot less social. 'I didn't know who he was when we met.'

'He knew who you were,' said Becks. 'I think we should ring that auction house.'

'Don't be daft,' Lou said.

'What was it called again?'

Lou was not co-operating.

Becks was Googling. 'Thompson Roddick. And you said it was a gold star with a school-tie-like ribbon, something from Europe, maybe the air force?'

'I can't remember,' Lou said.

'Too late, I am calling them … Hello there.' Becks put on a posh accent. 'I'm wondering if you have any World War Two medals. You do? Any gold stars? I believe some may have come in today. Thank you.' Becks raised her eyebrows, waited. 'You don't? Nothing new in today? No. Okay, thanks for your help.' She hung up and looked at Lou with a whole lot of told-ya-so. 'She did not take her grandfather's medal to the auction house. My guess is it's got a new hidey hole.'

'Or,' Lou said, 'she ran out of time and is going to take the medal and junk another day. Honestly, Inspector, you don't know him like I do. Check this show, *Sinister Sons*. You should watch it. Almost everyone they speak to says he's innocent. There are all these sleuths investigating and campaigning for him. Apparently he had twenty-three marriage proposals in prison.'

'There is no hope,' Becks said. 'We're fucked.'

'And there's no real evidence, just that he found them dead and that he was in debt. Seems to me they just pinned it on him because he was entitled and a gambler.'

'Fucking hell. I can never work out if you're pretending to be stupid or pretending to be clever,' Becks said, then raced off.

At the top, Lou lay on the grass beside her cousin, the fairy-tale city stretched out beneath them.

'It's not ugly, is it?' Becks said.

'It's not,' Lou said, although it wasn't sparking the joy it was yesterday.

'The landlord for our flat wants to let it longer term after the festival. What do you think? We'd need a month's rent and same again for the deposit, fifteen hundred each, soon as possible. There'll be gas and council tax and stuff too, a couple of hundred a month. There are loads of others in line if we don't want it. What do you say?'

'Of course,' Lou said. She still had three grand left after her crazy alcohol/drugs/gambling spree with Tim. That should be enough to keep her going till payday. And surely she'd clear enough to pay £1,700 a month for accommodation and bills. She probably should work that out. 'What about all the poor performers though? I can't live like that. I need my space.'

'After the festival Cam's going to go to Tuscany and the others are going back home,' Becks said. 'It'll just be us. I promise.'

'Yay,' Lou said, over-committed emotionally, worried financially.

'Okay,' Becks sat up. 'I get that you have a major horn for this murderer guy.'

'Not major. I can get out of it, easy. But I don't want to judge him yet.'

'You don't need to judge him, a judge already did that. He killed his parents. He did twelve years inside. He's a lifer. He's bad. In olden times if you killed a parent they'd sew you up in a leather sack with some live animals, like a dog and a snake and a monkey, then they'd throw you into the water.'

'You know the weirdest facts.'

'Whereas you go for fiction. This guy is not normal. He is not just a posh gambler. Also, he speaks a lot of shit. You are not intriguing. I bet your Google search was "Timothy Wilson + innocent."'

(It was, and so was the expression on Lou's face.)

'You've picked two arseholes so far in a failed attempt to

do better than your gorgeous mum. But two's not a pattern. You're not completely screwed yet. Put the cheat and the creep down to youth, but if you decide to have an affair with a double murderer, then…'

'You haven't even read anything about it. His sister says—'

'Stop! What batshit-crazy person would do what you are obviously considering doing? You don't know him, or his sister. Maybe they'll murder you together, boil you and share you for dinner. Get him out of your head. Hit yourself if he comes to mind.' Becks emptied her backpack onto the grass: cloudy lemonade, Anzac biscuits, lamingtons.

Lou nibbled an Anzac. Of course her cousin was right.

Becks was on her second lamington. 'If you don't want to leave the job, and I can't imagine why you would want to stay, but if you do want to stay, you have to tell your boss.'

'I will.'

'Promise?'

'I do, I will, tonight.' She meant it. She did. 'Will you please bake at least once a week?'

'If you do too,' said Becks.

'Deal,' Lou said. 'Ooh, I'll do pavlova, with strawberries.'

'And Flakes.'

'Obviously.'

They groaned from the binge for a while, then closed their eyes under the sun, the peace suddenly interrupted by

Lou punching herself in the arm. 'Damn it,' she said. 'Feels like I've got an all-day Viagra erection.'

'Hit yourself harder,' said Becks.

The guy on the camping mat had left, thankfully. Apparently Cam from Canberra kicked him out for contributing bugger all. Lou was starting to not-hate Cam from Canberra. She put the clothes rack between the two single beds for some privacy, and to discourage other campers. 'Hope you don't mind,' she mouthed to him, as he still had his noise-cancellers on.

He gave her the thumbs-up and took his earphones out. 'Ta for the review.'

She'd almost forgotten, she'd given his gig – as well as *Plath!* – five stars.

'Hilarious, loved it. A must-see,' Cam said. 'When did you come? I didn't see you.'

Lou sat on the end of his bed. 'I'm trying to stop lying,' she said. 'It's hard but here goes. I don't ever want to come to your gig. The seats look really uncomfortable, if you can even get one, and you'll point at me and say mean stuff, and even if you don't I'll worry about it the whole time. I know how funny you are. I've heard you read the set more than fifty times (she'd heard it once) and you're even funnier in real life.'

Cam smiled. 'I appreciate the review,' he said, then he put his earphones back in.

Too tired to get undressed, Lou lay on her bed and closed her eyes.

❁

She was asleep in one of her many childhood bedrooms, hugging her pillow. 'Rise and shine, Louise O'Dowd,' her father was saying. 'Louise O'Dowd, I'll say it over and over, I'll say it till you wakey wakey, Louise O'Dowd.'

No, she was in her new flat in Edinburgh. It was 8pm, but light outside.

She peeked through some clothes on her rail – Cam wasn't on his bed. First time for everything. The place was empty, everyone had gone off to perform. They were all night workers in this flat.

Cam had left a note in the (sparkling clean) kitchen: *I've made meals, no nuts in anything but lots of other shit, check the labels and help yourselves, Cam x*

The fridge was filled with takeaway containers with pretty labels on them – *Chicken Korma, Vegan Korma, Shepherd's Pie, Lasagne, Beef Vindaloo, Cous Cous and Goat's Cheese, Pad Thai* – ingredients all listed underneath. The chicken korma was delicious, just what she needed to face her first solo night shift.

CHAPTER TWELVE

When Lou arrived at the hostel, two MILFs were leaning on the gate.

The front door opened and a round woman shooed them – 'I told you to get away from here,' she said.

'He wants to see us,' one of the MILFs said.

'I don't care. Get or I'll call the police. Get.'

Eventually, they obeyed.

'You must be Lou,' the woman said, holding out her hand. 'I'm Jacky. Come in, come in. Can you believe those women? Murder groupies, honestly, they'll do anything for a piece of Norman Bates up there.'

'Norman Bates?'

'Right enough, he's probably more of a Ted Bundy. One got in through the attic the other week.'

Jacky was balding, fifty-something, and from the Borders. She read her handover notes in a suicidal monotone: 'In on time, in on time, one minute late, in all day, in all day. Tim had a date…'

Hang on, what, what, what? Tim had a date? Not just gruesome groupies but an actual date? How dare Tim have had a date.

'…Rob was home in Livingston for the day. Polly's coming in tonight to talk to you.'

'Me?'

'You,' Jacky said. 'Lunchbox had his Tinder date but he did not feel a connection. Light's not working in top stairway. Camera in bottom hall seems to have stopped flashing, which means it's not recording – no big deal, those cameras only work half the time, and no-one watches them except Polly to catch staff sleeping, and the police if someone kills someone.'

'Has someone been murdered here?' Lou asked.

Jacky yawned, didn't have time for stories. 'Nothing to report with Chuggy, he's been in a good mood considering it's the anniversary of his aunty Rita's heart attack. He made macaroni cheese for me for lunch, we watched *Bambi*. I'll be off then.' And she left.

Just as Rob's wife, Stacey, arrived. She was holding several paper bags filled with shopping. 'If it isn't the deer in head-lights,' she said.

Lou was not warming to this woman.

'I need to ask you something.' Stacey shut the office door and swiped her phone. 'Tell me honestly – this doesn't look anything like Rob, does it?' She showed Lou a photo of Rob.

Only it wasn't a photo, it was a photofit, on a Facebook alert, from Lothian Police.

WANTED FOR INDECENT EXPOSURE
DO YOU KNOW THIS MAN?

The photo (fit) was of a man in his thirties with the following attributes:

Blond messy hair, blond moustache, 5'8" approx 18 stone, large round stomach, blue eyes, left ear with several silver piercings. Seen last Saturday between 5.30pm and 7.30pm on various buses in and around Livingston and at Livingston Bus Station. He was wearing a red tracksuit, white trainers and a blue baseball cap.

'Was Rob in Livingston at these times?' Lou asked.

Stacey nodded sadly.

'Red tracksuit?'

Another nod, eyes getting wet.

Lou was managing to build a rapport with someone she absolutely hated. She was going to be damn fine at this gig. 'I've seen the trainers and the hat,' Lou said, handing Stacey her phone. 'Of course it's him. What are you going to do?'

Stacey recoiled, put her phone in her pocket. This was not the answer she had asked for. 'You would say that.' Her tone was suddenly sinister.

'What?'

'You've got it in for him. You don't like him, or me.' Stacey moved in on her, pinned her against the door. 'We don't like you either. We think you're a stuck-up, ignorant cow who has no business being here, doing this job, posh bitch.'

Lou, posh? She grew up in boxes. She was a classless Aussie. Oh no, did they think her accent was English?

'That's not him,' Tracy said, desperate to persuade herself. 'Five years inside that hell hole getting beaten up and spat at, then one year here getting poked and prodded and group-worked and made to talk about sex all the time, and I mean that's all they want him to talk about. He even has to do homework. They make him draw A3-size fannies, there's one on my wall. He never gets the bus, you know. He hates buses. This is bullshit. This is not him. You'd better forget you ever saw this or…'

'Or what?'

'Or I'll be really fucking angry. And when I get really fucking angry I rip out chunks of rosy cheeks with my teeth. Not one word about this, you hear me, headlights?'

Lou found herself hyperventilating against the office door. She could hear Stacey hollering up the stairs to her husband, then some muttering, the door opening, closing. It was Polly arriving, thank god. Lou had so many questions, so many things had already happened. She needed advice.

Polly came into the office and shut the door behind her. 'It's been quite a day,' she said, sitting at the desk. 'I was at the prison this morning. We have a new resident coming after Rob moves home on Tuesday. He's going to have a lot of challenges.'

'What did he do?' Lou said, taking the risk and the seat opposite.

Polly straightened her back and looked down at Lou. 'He "did" a lot of things. At eighteen he was a rugby champion, played for Scotland.'

'Oh.'

'I called this meeting…' (Did she?) '…to discuss your job description. Because I'm wondering where it says that you should toss people's belongings in binbags and call them rubbish?'

Oh dear, Lou was at a parent-teacher meeting again.

'Lunchbox's mother's remains were in the bag that you labelled "Games Room Rubbish".'

'I'm sorry,' Lou said, trying to remember anything remotely box-like. 'What were the ashes in?'

'A Mackies ice-cream tub.'

She remembered, the decision was quick. 'So sorry, I thought it was dirt.'

'Why would we keep a plastic tub of dirt in the games room?'

'That was my thinking,' Lou said.

'She loved Mackies, his mother.'

'Oh.'

'This is not your home,' Polly said. 'It *is* the home of these five men, however, and they have rights and they have personal belongings that are meaningful to them, if not to you. It's very odd behaviour, on your first night shift, and it makes me worry about your thinking processes. What were you thinking?'

Lou was thinking: this place is a pigsty and a disgrace. If she had to live here she'd turn to crime too. She was thinking Polly is ugly, ugly, and an arsehole. She was thinking: *Shit, I am my father*. She was thinking she must not hit Polly over the head with something heavy, the mouldy vase on the desk, for example. She said: 'I was thinking that morale would improve if the house was cleaner and more organised – like with a good scrub and clear-out, and with some systems in place for coats and shoes and crockery, for example, then the house might spark some joy for the people who live here.'

'Spark some joy?' Polly said, almost laughing. 'What do you care about pretty coats systems when your family died in a gas explosion and your uncle abused you for seven years?'

Who was she talking about?

'What does a chipped mug matter when your dad pushed a gram of coke up your anus before the family holiday in Spain?'

Lou didn't have an answer. She gulped, confused. It was a relief to see Stacey, who had barged in without knocking. 'Gotta go,' she said to Polly. 'Babysitter.'

The meeting was over. Polly was standing. 'Any questions overnight, call Neens at SWASOL. See you tomorrow.'

Stacey's parting look was comedy gold – over the top I'm-gonna-kill-you evil.

Lou never put up with this kind of bullying; she always had a good put-down at least. She wasn't sure how to handle the situation when she was being paid. Before losing the courage, she fired off an email to Polly:

Subject: Meeting Time, Urgent

Hi Polly, I didn't get a chance to talk to you tonight and it's urgent. It's about 1. Stacey's aggressive behaviour; 2. Allegation on Facebook re Rob; 3. Doug following me home this morning; 4. Timothy.

She didn't elaborate on the fourth point. Just finished with:

Can you please let me know when suits you to meet? Best, Lou.

It was 9.30pm when Lou realised she hadn't spoken to Doug as promised. She raced up to his first-floor room and knocked on the door.

'You may enter,' he said. He was lying in his bed with the duvet right up to his chin. *Hostel 4* was playing on his ancient television.

'How are you doing?' she asked.

'Good, good.'

'Did you talk to Euan?'

'Euan? About what?'

'About how worried you've been, the five thousand and everything.'

'Oh aye. Nah, it's all good, I was just paranoid.'

'So you don't want to make a plan?'

'Oh, I've made one.'

'Yeah?'

'Let me know if you or any of your flatmates want some cocaine, eh?'

'That's not appropriate, Doug.'

'I'm joking. I'm feeling much better. Thanks for checking on me. I appreciate it.'

He was probably stoned. She'd try him again later, the poor thing.

She wanted to head upstairs to Tim's floor, but stopped at the light switch on the landing, which she checked – it was indeed broken. She wondered who he'd had a date with, where they'd gone, what they'd done.

She made her way to the basement, where Rob was watching *Dexter* in the front row. The basement curtains were open. She could see legs walking by. She rushed over to the window, looked at the miniscule courtyard and the pavement above, which was at the perfect height for the viewing of legs, legs passing by, lots of legs. Rob was in upskirting heaven.

‘Shall I shut the curtains?’ she said. The street was busy tonight with all the clubs and pubs nearby. Thursday was party night. Or one of them. There would be so many drunk legs. She wondered if she was imagining things, if she was the creepy one, even to have the idea, even to notice the legs. The women had gone. No-one was in danger. She needed a coffee, some time alone in the office.

The Everything-You-Need-To-Know folder was so dull that she could not read it. She took a mental note of some of the headings – emergency contacts, fire procedure, complaint procedure – and set her chair up against the window, just like Neil did. She was already getting into the idea of quiet-quitting this job.

She wasn’t going to get into the toast and hot chocolate malarkey. Hot beverage management made her weak and slow. Also, timings were especially important when it came to the room checks. Just before ten past midnight, she looked at her phone as it counted down – three, two, one – then knocked on Lunchbox’s door.

He was standing on the bed, legs shaking, dressed only in his floral silk kimono, which was very loosely tied.

Lou did not look at his crotch area. She must not look there. ‘Noose, please,’ she said, and he handed her the rope, which was short, thin, untied, with no loop. 'Hook, please,' she said, and he handed her the wobbly, plastic, nonsense, piece-of-shit hook, the same as the one Neil took yesterday, only she didn't notice how flimsy it was at the time. This toy hook was supposed to somehow attach itself to the screw holes in the disintegrating plaster in the ceiling, which was completely out of reach, even when you're standing on the bed. Lunchbox was already getting boring. No way was she going to do any paperwork. Lou tucked him into bed and gave him a tissue for the tears. 'I'm sorry about your mum's ashes.'

'Fuck my cunt of a dead mother,' he said.

Wanting to move things on, Lou said: 'I hear you had a date.'

'It's not going to work,' he said, blowing his nose, 'the *plan*. There's no longevity.'

'Sorry, what?'

'If I do get a seventeen-year-old I fancy, it won't be for long. Six, twelve months max. I'll have to get a fresh one every six months, it's just maths. Where am I gonna get them all from?' He blew his nose again; hefty. 'Do you have any nieces, little sisters, do you know any fifteen-year-olds?'

'Don't you mean seventeen?' Lou said.

'Oh, Jesus Christ.' He lay on his side. 'Just let me die. I want to die.'

'Night,' she said, closing his door.

She knocked on Rob's door next. He was lying in bed watching *The Human Centipede*. He'd hardly made a dent in wrapping his vape bottles. There was a wedding photo on the bedside table. The filter didn't fix Stacey's face. Rob had nothing to report. He was going to nod off soon.

Doug was still hiding in his duvet. His mood had plummeted since her last visit. He hated living with fucking paedos. Where was his hot chocolate and raisin toast? Did he really have to get it himself? He was gonna get his limbs busted for five grand and he had no-one to turn to, nowhere to go.

She asked him if he wanted to talk about it.

He sat up. 'Yes. Your parents own two cars, then there's the caravan and the boat and the trailer.'

'How do you know that?'

'Online.'

'They're not online.'

'They might think they're not online. They're all over your Insta, so are all the rich, Aussie, artsy wanker pals you share that posh flat with. You could pull five grand out of a hat if you really cared about me, about whether my legs will be broken tonight or not. But you're not gonna bother your arse. You're just like everyone else. You don't give a shit. I don't want to talk anymore. I want to be alone,' he said.

Lou was happy to leave him alone. She was going to have to give up Instagram soon. Arsehole.

Chuggy Chatroom was in bed. 'How's your first proper shift?' he said.

'It's good, thanks. Can I please have a look at your phone and your laptop?'

His ancient laptop was for games and DVDs, not attached to the internet. She handed it back with a smile. His flip-phone, similarly, had no internet access. She checked his text messages – a few from his mum, one from a friend called Ben.

'Who's Ben?' she said.

'He's from AA. I'm his mentor. He needs a lot of support.'

She was now checking his phone calls. There were at least ten a day to and from Ben, ranging from between ten minutes long to two hours and twenty minutes.

'It can be difficult being the newbie,' Chuggy said, taking the phone back. 'Lonely.'

For a second she was tempted into this conversation. It *was* lonely. She needed so much help. And there was no-one.

'Do you want to talk about it?' he said.

She realised that he was trying to smell depression on her. That was his Viagra. It was why he loved *The Notebook* and *Beaches*, and people who loved *The Notebook* and *Beaches*. He was getting a tiny buzz talking to her. But he was wrong. She was not depressed. She was exactly the opposite. She was not manic either. She was happy. He could shut the fuck up.

She shut the door and added a couple of notches to Chuggy's score on the creepo-meter. He was now neck and neck with Lunchbox, Rob coming in a very close third.

CHAPTER THIRTEEN

Lou was standing at the foot of Tim's bed, trying to look professional as she scanned the room for cocaine or today's underpants or the stolen family jewellery or the gun.

'Good day?' she said.

'Yeah, good, thanks.' Tim was sitting at his desk, laptop now shut.

'Any gambling?'

'None.'

'Drugs?'

'None.'

She wasn't convinced. 'Have you murdered anyone?'

Tim didn't find this funny. She regretted saying it, needed to get her work head on. What could she see, what could she say? Ah, the bin was empty. 'Thanks for taking my things to the bin.' But she had said the wrong thing again – there were so many wrong things to say in this place – as they were both now thinking about her pants.

The green tin from Tavisdale was sitting on the chest of drawers, still locked. 'So what *is* in that box?' she said.

'Give you a tenner if you guess.'

'Just tell me.'

'I really want to know – no, I really need to know – what you think might be in the box,' Tim said.

'Okay,' she said, 'but this is not a bet.' She walked over to the chest of drawers, tugged at the little padlock and lifted the tin. It was heavy, not something that rattled or shook. 'Might be a gun,' she said, 'wrapped up in something.'

Tim cracked his knuckles.

Lou put the box back down on the chest of drawers, then went for it. 'Could be your mum's engagement ring, in there, the one with the sapphires and all the diamonds, or your grandfather's war medal – unless that was the one I found in Tavisdale. Which auction house did your sister take them to?'

'Thompson Roddick.'

'Did she?'

'It's the one she always goes to. I don't know.'

Back to the box. 'Or it could be a lock of hair from your beloved mum, may she rest in peace. If she hadn't died, everything would have been so different for little Timmy.'

His poker face was excellent. She hadn't even noticed him blink.

'Could be photographs of your dad and your stepmum with their faces scratched out in angry pen, all torn or burnt because you didn't love them, you hated them, you hated them so much you blew their heads off.'

He blinked.

'Or it could be photos of you and your stepsister Ruth getting fake married aged ten and twelve, and again aged fourteen and sixteen.'

He blinked.

'Or it could be the love letters you sent to each other at boarding school. Lou mimicked the voices of Tim and Ruth:

'"Dear Tim, I know it's wrong…" "Darling Ruth, how can it be wrong?"'

She had rattled him and she liked it. She did not want to stop.

'But if I was only allowed to make one guess, I would wager it's Nathan's birth certificate in that box, saying you're not his stepuncle, you're his father.'

'Jesus Christ.' Tim had heard enough. 'The tabloids didn't even go there.' He had an over-large set of keys in his pockets. One of the tiny ones opened the box. 'Family snapshots,' he said, holding the box upside down and letting the loose photos fall onto the chest of drawers. Some fell on the floor. All the photos were of smiling faces, none of them scrubbed out or burnt off. Tim picked up a handful, started sifting through them: His mum walking him in a pram … the new blended family at the castle wedding … him and Ruth swimming in the pond … Tim and his dad fishing … Christmas morning at Tavisdale. 'I can't make you believe me, you have to make your own mind up,' he said.

She wondered if there were tissues in Raymond the

backpack. Tim needed one. Perhaps she should give him a hug. She'd better not.

'I'm just trying to carve out some kind of life. Making a mess of things as usual.'

She decided to give him a professional hug, the kind she might give someone she didn't fancy. She patted his back, moved away. Mm, sandalwood. 'Like your new dressing gown,' she said.

'Thanks.'

'Which hotel?'

'Marriott.'

'From your date?'

'Is it a rule that I have to tell you about my dates?'

'I don't know the rules exactly.'

'Right now, you're supposed to check the room.'

'Right,' Lou said, opening the wardrobe doors (no women, only clothes). She shut the doors, turned around. 'I think I might be jealous,' she found herself saying, 'that you had a date. I want to know everything. Who was she and where did you go and do you like her and did she steal a dressing gown too and do you do this every day, with a different woman, like, what's your game?'

'Her name is Georgia, we met in a foyer, went to the Marriott, and it was fun. I like one-afternoon stands. I like making bets and getting room service. I haven't got a job, no money, not till the house sale is closed. I've found a temporary way to get what I want without hurting anyone and it's been fun.'

It was definitely jealousy that she was feeling. It hit her like it did with Haz and with Alan. She couldn't stand the thought of what happened in the Marriott.

'Not as fun as being with you, but that had to stop. Listen, I was in prison for twelve years. I was seventeen when I went in.'

'A virgin?'

'I've had some catching up to do. You're the only woman I've seen more than once. In the eleven months since I got out.'

Which meant he'd probably shagged and fleeced over a hundred women in eleven months. 'Tell me about your first girlfriend, Tanya. What happened with her?'

'I stole six hundred quid from her. She'd worked in the corner shop every Saturday and Sunday for years. She was saving for a car.'

Okay, so his story matched with Ruth's, again. And his answer seemed too awful to make up.

'Neil said you're in debt,' she said.

'About seventeen hundred,' he said.

'Who to?'

'Friends. Ex-friends.'

'Gambling?'

'Gambling. There'd be no new robe if you hadn't dumped me.' He stood, moved a step towards her. 'Undump me. There are so many things I'm trying to change about myself, that I'm trying to stop – the next bet, thinking about it all the time, every minute of every day, taking advantage of people, lying, hating myself for it – but I don't want to stop this. Do you? I'll be a normal human being again in one month, in my own flat. We can keep it secret till then. We won't be hurting anyone.'

Lou didn't reply. Instead, she wondered if his flat would be a traditional tenement with huge windows or one of those tiny concrete ones further out. Surely he'd get something decent with half the proceeds of Tavisdale. As long as he didn't fall out with Ruth; as long as she didn't find out that he was gambling again. A man yelled out the back. She looked out the window.

'What's that?' said Tim.

'Can't see anything. I'm going to go check. Stay here.'

Lou walked down to the basement and into the games room. All the bags she had neatly labelled had been split open. There was rubbish all over the floor and a huge angry felt-tip sign on one of the many grotty, flattened cardboard boxes: *DO NOT TOUCH*. She stepped over the broken games, empty bottles and jars, and all the rest of the junk. This place was defiantly disgusting, agonising, designed to mess with her head. She had to stop herself from ripping the sign into little pieces and taking it, and everything else, out with her to the bins.

There was no-one in the courtyard that she could see. The automatic light was so bright it probably woke up everyone. She came back upstairs and opened the front door to have a look out on the street.

Posh pastel guy was standing in front of her, on the pavement, staring up, his ginger cat in his arms. It meowed.

'You scared me,' she said.

'I was looking for Bertie,' he said, patting his cat.

'Is there something I can help you with?'

'You should get out of that place, just leave, you're not safe in there.' He crossed the road, went back inside.

A group of drunk women turned into the street. They were heading this way. Before going back inside, Lou realised that posh pastel had dropped his cat's tag with his name engraved on it: *Bertie*. Work backpack on, she left the door open, raced over to his door and popped the nametag through the letterbox.

The drunk women were in front of the house now. They were blocking her way, staggering, singing, loving each other. She should never have left the door open. As she made her way through the gaggle, she looked down into the basement. And there was Rob, in his front-centre cinema armchair, dick out, wanking like crazy at all the legs that were passing by. He looked up, spotted Lou, didn't quite stop what he was doing for a second, or even two.

The legs women didn't notice – thankfully. Lou waited

on the step until they had disappeared around the corner, then closed the front door behind her and took some deep breaths.

She heard a noise in the basement. Rob, she supposed. She wondered if her job description included confronting wanking sex offenders in basements and decided it probably did.

The noise was a voice, or two. Rob was not alone in the cinema room. She rushed down the stairs. One of the legs women must have come inside while the door was open. He had taken one of the legs women.

She listened at the door of the cinema room. The voices were quiet now. There was music. Perhaps Rob had just drugged his victim.

Lou still had Raymond (the work backpack) on. She could stab him with the noose knife. She could inject him with the naloxone thingy, although she had no idea what it would do to someone who hadn't overdosed. She could use her phone. She should, she should dial 999, now.

A scream in the cinema room made her jump. Without thinking, she kicked the door open.

There was no-one in the cinema room. *Alien* was playing. Lou turned it off, put the knife and the revival kit back in Raymond and headed upstairs to check the rest of the house. All doors seemed secure, all residents seemed to be in their bedrooms. She went back downstairs, into the office, and called Polly.

Polly didn't answer, so she left a message: *I need your urgent advice.* She sent an email, elaborating: *I saw Rob masturbating in the basement as women walked past. What should I do?* She emailed David Wilson, who had interviewed her. He was on annual leave for two weeks. Any urgent queries should go to Polly.

She took off the backpack, opened the drawer with the master key, turned to the Emergency Section of the folder. 'Where there is a life-threatening medical emergency or risk of imminent harm call 999. In all other cases, contact the manager.'

An hour later and there was no response from Polly. She rang Neens at the women's unit, but Neens couldn't talk because someone had stabbed someone and there were police everywhere because someone was in the attic with a machete.

Suddenly, Rob wandered in, all nonchalant in his tartan pyjamas. He sauntered round the room, fidgeting with bits of paper, a nervous toddler who might or might not be in trouble.

'We're going to need to talk about what just happened, but not now,' Lou said.

'What do you mean?' He didn't look at her.

'You know what I mean.'

'No, I don't,' he said, but his face was red.

As he left the office, her phone pinged – text message from an unknown number.

Are you okay? Tim

Of course Tim had more than one phone.

Can't talk, she messaged.

No worries. Just checking.

Actually, I really need to talk, she texted. *Can I call you?*

Her phone rang immediately. What a relief to have an ally on the inside. His voice worked better this way, sounded deeper, less posh, kinder. 'Are you okay?'

'This fucking place,' Lou found herself saying. She shut the office door, then the sleepover room door, and sat on the bed. 'It's crazy. You have no idea how much is going on.'

'I probably do,' he said. 'What, though? Did something happen, are you safe?'

'I'm not allowed to tell you stuff, probably, I don't know. I can't get hold of Polly though. No-one is ever around to help me.'

'Let me help. I'm coming down.'

'No, no, we need to be careful, keep separate. Just, let's just talk. This is nice.' She wanted to tell him about Rob. She knew she shouldn't. She did anyway. 'Rob just…'

'What? What did he do? Did he intimidate you? Where is he? Fucking arsehole. Where is he?'

'No, no, wait, listen, there has been no touching, he just creeps me out.'

'Are you safe?'

'Yeah, I am, promise.'

'I can hear Rob,' Tim said. 'He's back in his room. I'm coming down.'

'No, I'm fine. I'm following procedures, dealing with it. There's nothing to worry about.'

'I get it. Confidentiality. I wouldn't want you talking about me to anyone either. You are okay though?'

'Yeah, it's just … he's blah.'

'He's just a flasher, there's nothing to be scared of. He just sends old-fashioned dick pics. But I'm gonna keep an eye on him,' Tim said. 'I'll pop down later, okay?'

The most relevant section in the Everything-You-Need-To-Know folder seemed to be Incidents. According to the lengthy advice she should fill out a form. She took two from the relevant pocket. Then she took another one and began writing.

First, regarding Rob, from the Lothian Police photofit to the basement wank.

Second, regarding Tim, from when she realised she knew him to now.

She ripped this one up and filled out the incident regarding Doug instead. He had followed her home, stalked her family, made veiled threats…

And was now knocking on the office door. 'It's Doug, can I please come in?'

'Can't sleep?' she said, letting him in.

He took the seat at the desk opposite her. 'Feeling better. I've had a good think. I've got a plan.'

'That's good. What is it?'

'So my plan is to pay them the five grand. Then it'll be over. I'm clean for the first time in my life, so I'll get a job. I've got my forklift licence, or I'll have it soon. I've met this great woman, Carrie-Annie, fucking gorgeous. She's high up on the housing list.'

'Decent plan,' Lou said. 'But where are you going to get the five grand?'

'I'm going to ask you one more time. Please help me out. I'll pay you back.'

She took a sip of dodgy water from a grimy bottle. 'I don't have any money, Doug.'

'That's your answer?' he said.

'Yes.'

He stood, stretched. 'Goodnight.'

Lou was shaking. She needed someone to talk to. She could go upstairs, knock on Tim's door. It wouldn't be so wrong. Becks was Ms Eastern-Suburbs-Judgy-Bitch. She didn't know him – or the case – like Lou did. And this job didn't matter, not really. She was only twenty-three, for fuck's sake, truly free for the first time in her life.

Where can we meet here? she messaged.

Are you okay? Tim replied.

Yeah, just want to see you.

Top staircase lights are out, Tim typed. *There's a big cupboard, a box room with a bed in it, at the top, first right. The camera up here isn't working either but no-one's figured that out yet. I'll leave the light in the cupboard off, door ajar.*

Lou put Raymond on her back, locked the office door behind her, and walked up to the first floor. She could hear Chuggy Chatroom talking quietly on his phone, to his AA friend probably. Doug's light was on. She could hear him pacing up and down, probably wondering how to get five grand out of the new night worker. Lunchbox was the loudest. His wails followed her all the way up the narrow staircase, only fading when she got to the top-floor landing. Rob's room was straight ahead. She could hear him talking, she could hear Stacey talking. They were probably FaceTiming about what to do about the new night worker.

The door to the box room was ajar and the light inside was off, just like Tim promised.

'Psst. Here.'

She didn't allow herself to think. Why should she? She walked in and shut the door behind her.

CHAPTER FOURTEEN

Becks had managed to borrow a car and was beeping the horn at street level.

'Coming,' Lou yelled from the third-floor tenement window. Cam handed her some sandwiches ('You can't survive on cake'), and she ran down the stairs, dreading everything about the day ahead: the forty-minute drive with Becks, the two-hour walk up a hill, the one-hour picnic, the walk back down, the drive back home. Altogether too much time with Becks, who was turning out to be nosy and demanding again. Lou was never going to be able to avoid the subject of Tim. Last night! She'd never take it back, apologise for it, she'd probably think about it for the rest of her life.

Becks was rage-beeping. No wonder the ground-left neighbour was displeased.

'What on earth?' she said from her vestibule.

'Sorry, it won't happen again,' Lou said, rushing outside and jumping into the passenger seat. 'Drive I tell you,' she said to Becks. 'Just drive.'

It didn't take long to get out of the city and over the Forth Bridge. They were heading to a hill in Perthshire and so far, the country was giving the city a run for its money. *I'll see you one castle and raise you two lochs.* Becks was relaxing into the drive, which meant Lou was about to get grilled.

'How did it go, did you tell your boss?'

'I left her a voicemail, a text, an email. She is so hard to get hold of.' That wasn't a lie. 'I'm seeing her tonight at nine,' she said. Still not a lie.

'And you'll tell her then, that you have had a relationship with one of the inmates?'

'Residents.'

'Inmates.'

'I will. Honestly. It's at the top of my list.'

'And you won't go near him, like sexually? You didn't go near him, did you?'

'Course not.'

She lied. And there went the only friendship she had. She didn't want to be in the car with Becks. She didn't want to walk up a huge hill to eat lemon-meringue pie. She definitely did not want to share a flat with her for the next six months or more and was already hoping to find something cheaper. £1700! How did people get by in Scotland? She'd need another job. Maybe one of her colleagues would know someone with a spare room, by the sea perhaps, or in the Old Town. One of them might even have a bed or a sofa. It'd be fun to live with Neil. Or Euan, he seemed interesting. She didn't want to think too much about the flat in Leith that Tim might buy.

Lou kept up with Becks all the way to the top of the hill. She ate some lemon-meringue pie, then lay on her back and pretended to relax.

'Good, thanks,' said Becks, lying beside her.

'What?'

'My life, things are good.'

Lou was getting sick of Becks and her stroppy self-righteousness. She was feeling okay about lying to her.

'Thanks for asking,' Becks said.

'I'm sorry, you're right,' Lou said. 'How's it all going?'

'It's all going great.'

Okay, so she was going to have to sound really, really interested. 'What in particular? The play?'

'Yes, the play. And a hottie called Cal, they have tatts everywhere, every inch of their arms. But mostly the play. I've had calls from movie people.'

'No?' Lou was really interested now, if not really, really. Not enough for the single bed in that dark box room to fade.

'Guess who this is.' Becks put her hand to her ear and spoke in a deep Cate Blanchett voice: 'Hello, is that Becks? I hope you don't mind but I have tracked you down.'

'Nicole Kidman rang you?'

'Cate Blanchett, dick. Her people rang me. Her people's people in London, anyway, on Zoom.'

'That's incredible. Really?'

'Who knows. I'm meeting the London people after the matinee tomorrow. They want to do a deal.'

'Jesus, Becks, this is amazing. I am so coming too.'

'Yeah, yeah.'

'I am coming! I would not miss it. This is amazing.'

'I know.'

The drive home was fun for a while. They laughed, turned the music on, sang. Maybe Lou could maintain this friendship, despite the lie. It was only a small one. And she'd tell Becks soon enough, probably, if she needed to know.

There was a traffic jam getting back into the city. Lou fidgeted with the radio, opened the window. She wasn't going to get enough sleep. And the more she thought about it, the more annoyed she was at Becks. Lou had seniority. She did not appreciate being analysed and criticised and told what to do by her baby cousin.

'The landlord's holding the flat for us,' Becks said, 'but she needs the money by tomorrow or she'll go to the next in line.'

'I'll put it in when I get back,' Lou said. 'My phone's out of juice.'

It wasn't out of juice at all. She could have secured the flat then and there. She turned the volume down in case her phone made a sound. They were getting close to home – to her bed, to her pillow.

Guilt started to compete with irritation. 'I slept with Tim last night,' she said.

Becks tightened her grip on the wheel. 'At work?'

'Sorry I didn't say. I was scared to tell you because I know it's a complicated situation. It's just, I've never felt this way. It's the best thing that's ever happened to me. It's unstoppable.'

'I've heard all that before,' Becks said.

'It's different. And he moves out in a month. We're going to keep it quiet till then.'

Becks wasn't holding back with the sighs. 'So you're not going to tell your boss,' she said. 'You're not going to leave the job either. You're not going to stop this.'

'No, no, no.' Fuck her.

Becks curled her back and groaned. 'It's a pattern now, you have chosen your path. You'd rather have a toxic relationship with a parent murderer than a healthy friendship with a woman. I won't talk to you about relationships anymore.'

'Then I should find somewhere else to live after the festival.'

'Fine.'

'You always make me feel bad about myself,' Lou said.

'You always lie,' said Becks, double-parking by the flat. 'I'm dropping the car back, see you later.'

Lou hated being called a liar, probably because she was

one. 'Fine.' She slammed the door and watched her ex-friend drive off.

⁂

When Lou turned to go inside, Doug the drug dealer was sitting on the front steps.

'She looks nice,' he said. 'Becks, isn't it?' He held up his phone on Lou's Instagram page: a photo of Lou and Becks on Arthur's Seat. 'Where's she off to?'

Did this guy really have no-one else to stalk? Was she really going to have to delete her socials? He was getting scary. 'I'm calling the police, Doug.'

'I would really appreciate that,' he said, standing up, dusting off his pants, and walking off.

⁂

Cam was eating soup and a toastie in the kitchen. Lou took some into the bedroom, got into her PJs and blocked Becks's number and contacts. Immature, but satisfying. There were yellow roses on the side table. Cam had made the room cosy. In bed with her soup, she left another message for Polly, then rang Neens at SWASOL.

'Doug keeps following me home and asking me for money,' she said. 'What should I do?'

A baby was crying in the background. It was hard to hear Neens. 'Sorry,' said Neens, 'we found a newborn in the linen cupboard and we're trying to work out whose it is. Do you know why no-one's answering at the men's unit?'

'I don't,' said Lou. 'I'm sorry. I've been trying to get Polly. Should I call 999?'

In the background there was screaming, newborn and adult. '999 won't bother with us,' Neens yelled, 'unless someone is already dead, so if you're scared about Doug or whatever, give Mike a call. Mike Kearney – he's a local cop. He'll pop by, talk things over, show a presence. I'll text you the number.' The crying suddenly stopped. 'No, don't put the baby there,' Neens yelled to someone. The baby began howling again. 'Good luck,' she said, 'Fridays are always the worst.'

CHAPTER FIFTEEN

Lou had a great sleep and was clear-headed when she set off for work. This job was not worth worrying about. She didn't get paid enough to worry. Anyway, the local cop was going to pop in at 1am. He sounded nice. And Polly would have dealt with the Rob masturbation situation already. He might be in jail, fingers crossed. As for Tim, he'd be free in a month. They could hide it till then, easy peasy.

This was her third night shift. After tonight she had four whole days off. She should book a flight in the middle of the night, Copenhagen maybe. If Tim wasn't allowed to travel abroad, they could have brunch, do hikes, ride bikes. Maybe she could even try the bedroom. She could kick Cam out for the afternoon. He probably wouldn't mind.

It was Neil who answered the door.

'Hi, my darlin' how are you?' He had a lot to say when he shut the office door: 'She's downstairs in the games room waiting for you – and they're down there with her too.'

'Who?'

'Rob and his wife.'

'What?'

'I know, I know. She's fucked in the head. Don't take it personally. Remember everything – hang on.' He gave her a pad and pen. 'Take notes – then I can record it after too. Tell her you're taking minutes, she's terrified of those. And don't worry, you've done everything right. You've ticked all your boxes. Go, you'll be fine. I'll stay here till you're done.'

She remembered her father's advice as she headed downstairs: fear is good, fear is fine. Some of his lines were adapted from movies but his advice was always spot on. She welcomed the fear as she knocked on the games room door and renamed it 'Fuck You'.

The contents of the rubbish bags were still strewn all over one side of the games room, the *DO NOT TOUCH* sign ripped and stained with tea or coffee. Polly was sitting miles away, at the far end of the table-tennis table. Stacey was on her left. Rob on her right. The remaining chair was in front of Lou, opposite the very distant threesome. They could at least have removed the net.

'Take a seat,' Polly said.

Lou didn't want to sit down but she did. She put the pen and notepad on the desk: 'I'll take minutes,' she said.

Polly's lips were thinner than usual. The surrounding area was yellow. 'We won't be needing minutes.'

Lou didn't put her pen down.

'You've made a very serious allegation regarding Robert,' she said. 'Very serious. The consequences couldn't be higher.'

'I understand,' Lou said, writing the important words down.

'Please stop writing and listen,' Polly said. 'What I need to know is this: what were you doing outside the building last night?'

This was a more serious ambush than she expected. Fear is fine. Fear is Fuck You. 'It's all in the handover notes,' Lou said.

'If you saw him, it must have been from outside, on the street. That's strictly against the rules, unless there is a fire. Was there a fire?'

Stacey couldn't help herself, she'd been itching to speak since Lou arrived: 'She made it up. She's got it in for him.' Her fists were white. Even her boobs looked angry. (Lou wished she would show less of them.) 'She's always had it in for him.'

'Thing is,' Polly said, 'I've been talking to Rob all day and he says he did not do it, he's adamant.'

So that's where she'd been all day.

'It's bullshit,' said Rob. He had his head down – the naughty toddler who might or might not be in trouble – hadn't looked at her once.

Lou was beginning to seethe. 'Forgive me, I'm confused. Which incident is bullshit, Rob – you masturbating all over Livingston buses last weekend or you upskirting and masturbating in the basement last night?'

'Buses?' Polly said.

Lou held her phone up with the police alert and the

photofit Stacey had shown her,. It could not look more like the real Rob. '"*WANTED FOR INDECENT EXPOSURE*",' Lou said. 'On buses in and around Livingston. Stacey didn't show you this? You just showed me it, Stacey?'

Rob looked at his wife accusingly. Had she really shown this to the night worker?

It only took two seconds for Polly to find it on her Samsung. 'That could be anyone,' she said, putting her phone down. 'Also Rob doesn't like buses.'

'Exactly,' said Stacey.

Rob shook his head to confirm that he had an active dislike of buses, wouldn't wank anywhere near one.

Polly was good at pretending to be in control. This was her house. She was in charge. 'Robert has worked so hard for six years. I've never seen anyone work so hard.'

Lou had little interest in taking on this battle. She was on automatic pilot, taking notes – and thinking about Tim.

'I'm late for handover with Neil,' she said. 'Is that everything you wanted to say to me, that I'm a liar, and that Rob's not offending all over the place?'

It was wonderful seeing the three of them speechless.

'Okay then,' Lou said. 'I've taken a note of this discussion, I'll add it to the rest. Shall I shut the door behind me?'

No-one answered.

'I'll shut it,' she said, and did.

CHAPTER SIXTEEN

The table-tennis meeting sounded even dodgier when Neil dictated Lou's notes into his phone:

'Polly's initial response to the allegation was to blame the new night worker – that she could be in trouble for leaving the building and that this was the major issue. (NB: The night worker had heard a noise and had good reason to go out the front door and check, as per handover notes.) For the rest of the meeting, Polly defended and colluded with the resident, for example, saying "I've been speaking to Rob all day and he is adamant he did not do it." (NB: Polly did not reach out or respond to the numerous messages from the night worker regarding the incident, instead spending all day hearing Rob's version of events.) When shown a photo of Rob and a Wanted for Indecent Exposure post, Polly argued that this could not be Rob as "he doesn't like buses".' Neil stopped recording and checked Lou's handwritten notes. 'She actually said that…'

Lou nodded. 'Explain her to me. I don't understand.'

'What created Polly?' Neil said. 'I ask myself that a lot. First off, I think she's titillated by bad boys, or shit guys, as I prefer to call them. I saw her cross her legs when she was reading Rob's indictment one morning – the ugly offence, don't make me say what he did. She loves to talk over the details with them for hours – offence accounts, over and over: "what did you do then, what did you do then, tell me what you did then, let's analyse this". It's easy to find yourself being in awe, even colluding with the guys, by the way. Be careful of that. One small lie, one small omission, seemingly too insignificant to think about, then bang, you're on their team. This is an unusual environment. You're in a house with a lot of rules everyone knows about, and a lot of rules no-one knows about. Like any other house, we're a family, and I'd say Polly's the daddy. She's an angry fucker, probably had no mates at school, sat in the corner getting mad because everyone was happier than her. She's a drinker, one of the lads, on the side of the downtrodden, the misunderstood, the criminally virtuous, the sexually deviant. Also, she wants results: good stats, low rates of reconviction. She can't have breaches and recalls all over the place, she'd lose the funding.'

Lou was finding this hard to listen to and wanted Neil to stop. Polly was horrendous. Polly was Lou. Polly was not Lou. Lou could never be Polly.

'She was moved here from a senior social-work job. God knows what she got up to in her last workplace. A lot of power, senior social worker in criminal justice. I tell you, she did something bad to wind up here. But they didn't realise what they handed her. Here, she's not only a member of the scariest gang in town, she's the gang leader. We get in the way. She does not want staff. Every team meeting we have, which isn't often, she gets the angriest resident to come along and yell at us for thirty minutes. She always has a favourite yeller by the way. Rob this year, Oliver last year, used to yell about dishes and room checks. She keeps their families on side – which is a good plan FYI. Oliver and his girlfriend hid in her allotment shed for a week when the cops were after them.'

Lou could hear Polly and Stacey. They were talking in the hall, opening the front door. She and Neil watched, relieved, as the two women walked down the street together.

'Does she shag them?'

'Rob, Stacey, Polly. I am not going there, I am not imaging that.' Neil scrunched his eyes shut, hummed and put his hands over his ears. 'Oh my god, who'd get shoved off the bed in that threesome?'

Rob must have gone upstairs. He'd be avoiding the basement from now on, surely. Lou said her goodbyes to Neil and closed the front door. Eleven and a half hours to go, then four days off. She could do this, especially with Timmy the Kid upstairs in his tiny little dressing gown. Before she left this morning, she'd thrown the Marriott one out.

Lou had a look at Neil's handover notes.

Rob (flasher) *out and about with Stacey* (scary wife) *all day. Lunchbox had another Tinder date with a seventeen-year-old and it went well, back since five.*

Tim had a parole appointment then went house hunting (Ooh, where?) *and shopping with his sister, been in since 8.30pm.*

Doug was in a much better mood, spent most of the day out and about, still due back.

Chuggy says he was at an AA meeting at 1pm (he was not able to confirm location) *and then again at 3pm* (ditto), *in for the night at five.*

Lou knocked on Doug's door. No answer. When she turned around, a teenage girl was kissing Lunchbox in the hall. His silk kimono was not quite tied shut. His chest hair, grey, unlike the dyed-black shagpile on his head, was even more abundant than Lou realised. He had his lift shoes on and was the same height as the wee girl and therefore able to tongue wrestle with comfort. Lou was witnessing something truly gross, clearly immoral. Sadly, it was probably legal. He had a whole heap of poky tongue. For the sake of her stomach, she had to intervene.

'Sorry, who are you?' Lou asked.

'This is Amanda,' said Lunchbox. 'She's just leaving. See you tomorrow, honey,' he said, kissing her on the lips and shutting himself in his room.

'Polly let me in,' said Amanda.

'Right. Sorry. How old are you?'

'How many people have I had to tell this today, Jesus. I'm seventeen. I can do what the fuck I like.'

Lou followed her down the stairs to the front door. 'Have you Googled him?'

'Mind your own business,' said Amanda. 'Age isn't everything. You're prejudiced.'

At the door, Lou noticed Amanda's shopping bag, which was full of goodies. There might have been a couple of soft toys in the mix. 'What did he give you?'

'Fuck you,' Amanda said, walking off as fast as she could.

Lou yelled after her, 'Google him.' When she shut the door behind her, she noticed an angry Lunchbox at the top of the stairs, his legs wobbling with rage not frailty. It was time for the safety of the office.

At 9.45pm everyone was in but Doug. If he didn't get home in fifteen minutes, she'd have to follow a procedure called 'Breach of Curfew'. This involved phone calls and reports and meetings and the reading of pages and pages filled with long sentences that made no sense. The guidance even had made-up words, like 'outwith', and typos like: 'the worker should speak *to* their report.' She decided that if Doug didn't get home, she'd ring her new cop pal. She wouldn't bother

reading this crap. There was no point contacting Polly, either. Or Neens at the women's unit – god knows what hell Neens was going to endure tonight: a fire, perhaps, or a mass suicide.

She heard the front door close at 9.57pm, but by the time she got to the foot of the stairs, Doug was nowhere to be seen. Then suddenly, someone was knocking.

It was a police officer. A mean one. 'Is Doug Simpson in?' he asked.

'Actually I'm not sure, sorry, I'm just on shift. Are you Mike?'

'I'm DC Fisher.' He showed her his ID. 'Did he come in just now? He was just ahead of us.'

'I was in the office, I don't know for sure.' She should have added that she did just hear the door; that she did assume Doug just came in. She wasn't sure why she didn't.

'Can I come in?' DC Fisher asked.

'Of course.'

A second cop was behind him. The two of them started up the stairs. 'I don't envy you, doing this job,' the mean cop said. 'This still his room?'

'Yes,' Lou said.

The police officer knocked on Doug's door, then knocked again.

Eventually, Doug opened up, rubbing his eyes, dressed in his PJs. 'What is this?'

'When did you get in?' the police officer asked.

'Ages ago. I've been asleep.'

'In your shoes?' Doug had trainers on.

'I put them on to answer the door. These floors are freezing.'

Everyone except Doug was now looking at the shag carpet.

'Can we have a look in your room? … What's that in your bed?' said the police officer, looking at a lump under the duvet.

'Have you got a warrant?' said Doug.

'Fine,' the cop said, shutting the door and heading back downstairs, his silent partner in tow.

DC Fisher had a parting speech for Lou. 'You shouldn't be working in this place with these people. He robbed two houses tonight. Simpson, one of the owners, is in an ambulance. They'll get him on CCTV. We'll come knocking again. In the meantime, keep an eye out for anything in his room for us, hey? Like phones, wallets, purses, jewellery. Good luck. Fridays are mental.'

When the police officers were out of view, Lou raced straight up the stairs to Doug's room.

'It's Lou. They've gone.'

'Come in,' he said.

He was lying in bed, duvet to his chin. His trainers were on the floor. There was some blood on one of them. Or maybe it was ketchup. 'Have you got something under your duvet?' She was looking at the conspicuous lump at Doug's feet.

'Just me.' He reached down and pulled out a pillow. He was tearful, jerking his head to look out the window every few seconds, smarting at every tiny sound.

'How can I help?' Lou asked, 'apart from money. I don't have any of that and if I did, I wouldn't give it to you.' She mustered her mother, sitting by her bed, listening. 'You've had a bad day, tomorrow will be better.'

'I just need to pay them back, then everything would be okay.'

'I can't help you with that. What about your family?' Lou regretted the question. They might have all died in a gas explosion. Or his father might be in prison for packing a gram of cocaine into his boy's anus on the way to the airport.

'My dad's been inside most of my life,' he said. 'I get a card sometimes at Christmas. Mum's a heroin user, mental-health problems, hep C, COPD, beautiful person. She's in a homeless hostel at the moment. Fucking rent, man, who can pay all that? She knows when I need taken out for a walk. We talk every day, tell each other everything. I don't know what I'd do without her. We only have each other.'

'You an only child too?'

'Yeah, now. My brother died six years ago from misadventure and my sister killed herself in Greenock.'

Oh my lord. 'When?' What a stupid question: *When?*

'Last year, just about to get out, too, she did it with a sheet, and the radiator, took her ages. She was always determined, about everything.'

'Sorry but what is Greenock, a prison or a place?'

Doug laughed, for some reason.

'I am so sorry,' Lou said. She ran out of words after that, pretended the pause was deliberate. Poor Doug. 'Do you have friends you can turn to?'

'They're risk factors. If I see them, I use. If I use, I deal and I steal. I'm trying not to go back to that again.'

'What about Carrie-Annie?'

'Found out she's shagging her ex-stepfather.'

Goddam, this guy was unlucky. Lou switched the television to a cake-decorating show and left Doug staring at it. She'd check on him again at midnight. As she left his room, she heard a buzz coming from under his duvet, and not from the phone on his bedside table. She decided to ignore it for now.

Lunchbox was standing on the landing, tiny, white, shoeless legs poking out of his silk kimono. 'Who do you think you are?'

Lou didn't answer.

'Do you even realise who you're talking to right now?'

So far, Lou wasn't talking to anyone. She was taking the high road rather than pointing out that she'd never even heard of the old codger. He wasn't important; his songs didn't make it to Australia.

'I don't appreciate you scaring her off like that, you have no right. She's seventeen, perfectly legal.'

'I'm not talking to you about this here,' Lou said, heading down the stairs.

'She's seventeen. You have no right, idiot,' Lunchbox yelled after her, his tiny little legs wobbling with rage.

In the office, she took her own advice and Googled 'Lunchbox'. There were pages of headlines, old and new:

'Don't Forget To Pack your Lunchbox – Paedo Legend Found Guilty on Three Counts of Child Rape'

'Rockstar Sobs as Judge Locks Him up for Fourteen Years'

'Most Hated Man in Scotland Rumoured To Be Living in Glasgow'

'Lunchbox Targeted by Aberdeen Vigilantes'

'I was eleven years old,' says victim. 'We were not in a relationship, I was a child, and he ruined my life.'

'Paedo Lunchbox Released after Serving Just Seven Years'

Lou had been scratching her arm too hard, there were marks. She was sleeping over with the most disgusting person in the universe. She could hear him crying upstairs.

He probably had his door open so it'd carry. She moved over to YouTube to watch a far more likeable resident.

> 999 Operator: Stay on the phone please, Timothy, there's help on the way.
>
> Timothy: I will. Please, please hurry.
>
> *[Glass smashing.]*

CHAPTER SEVENTEEN

PRESENTER: As the only child of a wealthy Scottish family, little Timmy was a shy toddler, often seen in family photos clutching his mother's leg.

Family Friend: Wendy adored being a mother and Timmy was such a happy little boy, just the cutest.

PRESENTER: Timothy's parents were both from prominent distillery-owning families and he wanted for nothing. His early childhood was blessed with green fields, rolling hills and an abundance of love.

Family Friend: The three of them were always playing games on the walk to school, like I Spy. I couldn't help but smile when I saw them.

PRESENTER: Things could not have been more perfect for the Wilson family until one day...
[Sound of car screeching.]

Primary Teacher: I had to tell little Timmy. His father was too distraught.

Lou looked up from her phone. Tim was standing on the other side of the desk.

'Personally I'd recommend the version on the *Killer Kids* series, the re-enactors are top notch.'

'Sorry.' She turned her phone off.

'Don't be. Ask me anything, let's talk about it, we can watch a show or two together.' He took a seat.

'Not here.'

'This is the confession desk. Everyone spills their guts here, even when there's an audience. It's not just appropriate for us to talk about my offending behaviour, it's expected.'

She supposed it was but it was awkward. She didn't know where to start.

'Want to play cards?' Tim said, opening the pack on the desk. 'Gin Rummy, no betting.' He shuffled and dealt, soon absorbed in the game. 'It's a weird power shift. You're my prison guard now. And I get the feeling you think I'm evil.'

'I think there's around a fifty-percent chance.'

'You're happy to sleep with someone who you believe as likely as not murdered his parents?'

She couldn't possibly be happy about that, he was right. 'Okay, forty-five percent. Were you violent in prison?'

'I was punched a couple of times, fought back with money and contraband, mostly, thanks to Ruth.'

'And before prison, there was the headbutt. Any other times?'

'I'm a posh kid from Fife, I went to boarding school, I have an English accent, I like the banjo … Let's just say I can defend myself. Ten of hearts, jack of hearts, queen of hearts.' He laid his cards down. He was going to win.

'Tell me about gambling then,' Lou said, laying down three fives.

'I've always been competitive.' He added his five to hers, then an ace, a two and a three.

'No?!' Lou said.

'As a kid I did every sport: golf, tennis, football, hockey, curling.'

'Curling?'

'There's ice, a rock, and a broom. I'll take you one day. I was always into watching sports too, going to the Kelso races with Dad, to the footy with my mates. It got bad at uni, mostly online, although I did make the journey to Dundee casino every weekend. Before the end of the second term I'd spent all my grant, sublet my digs, maxed out credit cards and borrowed from some scary rich Americans from the sailing society. I was dossing on sofas, drinking, taking coke.'

'Are drugs and alcohol big problems then?'

'No, they just power the buzz a bit more. It's gambling that's the problem. It's a brain disorder, I'll never have any control over it.'

'So both our brains are fucked. What is it I have again?'

'Dissociative disorder.'

'I don't think I have that. Gin.' She put the rest of her cards down.

'I did not see that coming.' He studied the cards, packed them up, took her hand. 'We've got four weeks, twelve shifts. We can do this. While we're in here together, we look after each other. I won't let anyone scare you.'

'Any new dressing gowns today?' Lou said.

'No, and there won't be again. By the way, the cameras down here are out. Come.' He took her hand and walked towards the sleepover room.

She stopped him before they reached the bed. The camera wasn't flashing, still broken. She closed her eyes, got lost in the kiss for a while. When she finally opened her eyes again, she couldn't be sure how long Doug had been standing there.

'Holy shit, sorry,' said Doug. 'I was just – never mind, sorry I'll go…'

Great, Lou thought. 'Now he's gonna blackmail me. He's gonna use this to get the money he needs.'

'Don't worry about him,' Tim said. 'He's a good guy, we're mates. I'll go talk to him now. See you at room check.'

This job was getting very complicated. Out of the five men, two had personal information on her and two had a vested interest in shutting her up. She was starting to feel quite fond of Chuggy Chatroom, who hadn't done anything to concern her. Yet.

She wasn't going to worry about Doug blabbing: *Guess what, I saw the night worker kissing the murderer!* No-one would believe the poor guy. If they did, Lou would argue or leave, whatever. Fuck them. Fuck it. Continue to fuck Tim. So far, it seemed no-one expected her to be good at anything, or to actually do anything. The 'work' they talked about on their website was nowhere to be seen. What work was she doing with these men? She was no more than the lowliest of prison guards in the scariest of wings. She had no uniform, no snazzy belt kit with weapons inside and not a single colleague at hand.

She found herself scrolling the search results for 'Timothy Wilson' (minus the '+ innocent'). There were fan clubs, crime writers who thought he was innocent, podcasters who disagreed. There were about ten television programmes and endless blogs and articles:

'Top Ten Myths about Timmy the Kid'. (1: He is not violent. 2: His relationship with his stepsister is normal. 3: He is rich. 4: He does not know where the murder weapon is.)

Lou stopped reading at 5: He is a virgin.

'New Evidence Blows Tavisdale Case Apart'. (There did not seem to be any new evidence.)

'Justice for Elvin and Meredith Wilson, R.I.P.'.

'Dapper Tim Rejects 123 Proposals from Prison Cell'.

Lou landed on the most recent documentary, made just prior to his release eleven months ago (*My Brother the Victim*).

Interviewer: Despite the damning circumstantial evidence, Ruth Wilson, now thirty-one, remains her little brother's biggest defender. In this exclusive interview she argues that her brother is not a murderous monster but an innocent victim. Ruth, welcome, and thanks for sharing your story with us. Can you start by describing your childhood with Tim?

Ruth: I didn't expect to like Tim at first. I was eleven, he was nine. Our parents had fallen in love during a convention in London. I was transported from the big city to a spooky ten-bedroom mansion in the countryside of Fife with animals everywhere and a new little brother. There were no neighbours for miles, no-one else to play with. I had planned on resenting and ignoring Tim, till I saw his little face. I couldn't help but smile. Huge toothy grin, cutest kid in the world, gave me a hug and wouldn't let go.

Interviewer: And how did you get on with your new stepfather, and how about Tim, how did he get on with your mother?

Ruth: Our parents were having the love affair of the century. Nothing existed for them but each other. So Tim and I stuck together. We had adventures. I never laughed so much. He was a caring, beautiful little boy. When we were sent to boarding school – ten and twelve, we were – we wrote to each other once a week, counted the days till our holiday adventures in Tavisdale: fishing, hunting, horse-riding, racing, playing cards.

Interviewer: Playing cards?

Ruth: I regret that we played cards so much.

Interviewer: Are you saying you were neglected by your parents, both of you?

Ruth: No, I'm not saying that, no more than other families like ours.

Interviewer: You mean wealthy families.

Ruth: I do, yes, with parents who expect nannies, boarding school, summer camps. Mum and Dad were not active parents, but they were good people. They loved us and wanted what was best for us. They must be so angry up there. Someone killed them. It was not their little boy.

Interviewer: How did they react when you got pregnant? You were just sixteen, is that right?

Ruth: They were angry. They're traditional. They threatened to take me off the will.

Interviewer: They seemed to do this – they threatened to

take Tim off the will, didn't they, just before they were killed? Because he had gambled his entire student grant away, correct?
Ruth: Yes.
Interviewer: And because he was subletting his student digs in St Andrews, couch-surfing all over the place?
Ruth: Yes.
Interviewer: And because he had accumulated credit-card and other debts amounting to seventy-five thousand pounds?
Ruth: Yes. No, they did it all the time, ever since I was sixteen. I was off the will for a couple of years, till they fell in love with their grandson. It was a parenting tactic, a threat. We made a deal early on, Tim and I. We would always share, no matter what the will said in the end. He had nothing to gain by killing them.
Interviewer: Except that he thought he might get the money straight away.
Ruth: They would have given it to him, if he asked. He did not need to hurt anyone. He would never hurt anyone.
Interviewer: He was found guilty, Ruth, he's been sentenced, he's even done his time.
Ruth: They say he snuck out of the gatehouse in the middle of the night, killed them, came back in. Have you seen the gatehouse? It's tiny. I would have heard him.

Interviewer: If you found out for sure that he did do it, would you still support him?

Eventually, she answered.

Ruth: He did not do it.

Someone was pounding on the front door. Jesus, she was easily scared in this place. She was coming, she was coming, they could stop with the pounding. It was 11.30pm – Mike Kearney was ninety minutes early.

'Lou, hey, I'm Mike,' the cop said. 'Any chance of a cuppa?'

Mike Kearney had a quiet voice that he used a lot. He was on his second cup of tea now, and talking about his brother, who lived on the Gold Coast.

'Do you go water-skiing?' he asked her.

'No,' she said.

He seemed shocked and disappointed by this. His nephew lived in Noosa and started every morning with a surf. 'You must miss surfing,' he said.

'Yeah.' She never went surfing, it was pointless, but this was the answer he wanted. She was finding it hard to concentrate on this endless small talk. She kept looking at the door, smarting at every outside noise. It might be Rob. He might have a story to tell, about the new night worker. Or it could be Tim, walking into the office in his tiny dressing gown at any moment, 'Hey baby, where were we?' Or perhaps Doug would come down and tell the tea-drinking officer what he just saw. Maybe Tim and Doug were fighting up there, one of them dying, they might stumble into the office covered in blood and it would all be because of her.

'I'd better head,' Mike said.

Thank god.

'Pubs are closing. How 'bout I follow you round on the room-check first, let the guys know who's on whose side.'

Thankfully, Kearney stayed in the hall the whole time, but all the men obviously sensed his presence. She'd never seen the residents so quiet and obedient. Doug was in bed, duvet to chin. Lunchbox wasn't pretending to try and kill himself. Chuggy was on speaker phone to his AA friend, Ben, who sounded young and was sobbing. Chuggy hung up for Lou to check his devices.

'You've been speaking to Ben for hours,' she said. 'Is he okay?'

'He's really not,' Chuggy said.

'How old is Ben?'

'I shouldn't have even told you his name, it's not allowed.'

'How old?'

'He's twenty-four. It's not me who's the paedo.'

'You shouldn't be mentoring Ben,' Lou said. 'It's the

wrong job for you. I'm going to make a note of this and bring it up with Polly.'

'She's a big supporter of AA,' he said.

'I bet she is,' said Lou.

Rob was in his bed watching telly, and so was Tim. Phew.

'All quiet. Looks like you're going to have a fabulously dull night,' Mike said. 'I'll pop in again next week.'

Please don't, she thought, but when she shut the door and stood in the hall, the house seemed safer than it ever had. The men were all in their rooms for the night. She could sit on the sleepover bed and watch *I Should Be Dead*, maybe the one about the father and son who go a-bonding and get stuck in a cave.

Tim had messaged: *He's not going to tell anyone, all good. x*

She was sitting almost upright on the sleepover bed, watching a delirious dad fall even further into the crevice, when Tim appeared, dressed in flannel pyjamas and holding two mugs of hot chocolate.

'Hey. You're not sleeping are you? Naughty, naughty.' He sat on the bed beside her, handed her the drink.

'Doug's not a problem?' she asked, paranoid, rightly, at last.

'Not at all. He's a really lovely guy, just has shit luck.'

'He didn't seem surprised to see us together just now. Does he know about us? Have you two been in cahoots all along?'

'No, honey, I wouldn't tell that nutjob anything.'

'You said he's a lovely guy.'

'He's a lovely nutjob. Shall we do something outside tomorrow? How 'bout the Falkirk Wheel?'

A day trip sounded grown up and tiring. She'd done too many with Becks this last week. 'We'll see,' she said, pulling the lumpy backpack out from under her pillow and sitting it beside her. The neighbour's cat was purring outside on the window ledge. 'Hey Bertie,' Lou said, sipping the hot chocolate.

Tim shut the curtains, washed his hands in the grotty kitchenette sink, dried them with a crusty tea towel and tucked her in. 'Don't fall asleep,' he said, kissing her forehead, taking her drink.

She shut her eyes. 'As if.'

CHAPTER EIGHTEEN

She was thirteen, snuggled under her floral duvet, thin pillow under her head, in one of her many childhood homes. Her parents were having breakfast in the kitchen, a ritual they both labelled 'leisurely'. She could hear her mum placing her dad's favourite china plate underneath her dad's favourite little bowl, the perfect size and shape for the right amount of All-Bran. Cutlery jingled, the microwave pinged, the kettle boiled, the toast popped. It was time for Father to make his way to the breakfast table where Mother would serve him.

'Why do you put up with him?' Lou was saying, the women of the house now clearing up after brekky.

'I love my life,' her mother was saying, 'and I love your father. The sooner you realise that all relationships with men are transactional, the better. You've just got to make the best deal possible. Is there a cat in here?'

She was in bed in a beach-view apartment. A cat was meowing, or was that Alan Bainbridge? She was making money by lying still, doing nothing, the best deal ever. 'Don't move,' Alan was saying. 'Don't move don't move don't…'

No, she was in the sleepover bed in Edinburgh, must have nodded off. She really was terrible at this job.

The meowing was coming from outside. Bertie, and he sounded distressed. Lou reached for the bedside lamp, but it wasn't there. That's right, she'd moved it to the kitchen during her manic cleaning spree.

Meow.

She stubbed her toe on the way to the window and hopped in pain, grabbing the curtain for balance and ripping a few rings from the rickety metal pole. Startled, Bertie pounced from the outdoor windowsill onto the front step and raced across the road. Posh Pastel opened his front door to let him in. Lou waved. He didn't wave back.

The streetlamp was bringing light in, but it was taking its time. Sliding her hand along the wall, she found her way to the light switch. It wasn't working. She tried to open the door to the office. It was stuck. She turned the handle again and pulled, confused as she remembered leaving it open, but it would not budge.

Becks was right, she was an idiot. She had fallen asleep on duty and somehow locked herself in. She always made dumb mistakes. Her eyes had adjusted to the light, and she could see that there was no bulb in the ceiling. She searched the kitchenette units for a replacement – none.

She pulled at the curtains to open them fully. They fell to the floor and the metal pole followed, just missing her arm.

Where was her work phone? She'd left it on the bedside table. Where was her tablet? She shook the duvet and the pillows, lifted the mattress, swiped her hands on the floor. She crawled around the tiny rectangular room but could find nothing but grot. Raymond the backpack was gone. The work Blackberry, gone. Her tablet, gone. She couldn't find her leather bumbag either, with her Visa card and her house keys and her personal iPhone.

She had not locked herself in. Someone else had, and they'd also stolen her belongings.

It might be a joke, she thought. Tim pulling a prank, perhaps. He might walk in any second and say 'Gotcha!' It wasn't funny.

She could hear a noise, but she couldn't work out where it was coming from – the cinema room below, perhaps. Maybe Rob had locked her in so he could enjoy his nightly viewing pleasure without intervention. Indeed, a group of young people were walking by now – one of the clubs must have just closed. Lou tried to open the window, but it required a key. She knocked on the glass but her fists hardly made a sound. The Georgian sash window was reinforced with an inner window, which was thick, double glazed, unbreakable, sound-proof. Too late, the clubbers had walked by. She looked across the road at the lines of windows in the terraced houses, dozens of them. She could not see one face.

She pulled and pulled at the door handle to the office.

She kicked the door, got nowhere, and regretted making a noise. If she kept quiet, perhaps she could still get away with this. There might be an ending where no-one found out what a dickhead she was; where someone quietly unlocked the door and let her out; where she didn't appear on the front page of *The Age* as the sex worker who was taken hostage.

Lou knocked tentatively … 'Hey, is someone out there?' On her hands and knees, she scoured the floor again, finding nothing but a butter knife and something very sticky that was now all over her jeans and hands.

It was most likely to be Doug. A robbery. Doug didn't scare her. He might not come back anyway. He probably took her stuff, locked her in and ran away. The best thing to do was wait to be rescued.

But who by?

The screws holding the door hinges were impossible to reach. Lou started on the smaller ones around the door handle, using the flat end of the knife to loosen them one at a time. Just one more focused turn … she pressed hard, harder, and turned.

The blade of the knife broke, slicing her finger. Blood spurted all over the door and all over her T-shirt. She put her finger in her mouth, sucked. As she was wrapping the wound with a tea towel, the door handle fell to the ground and a shard of light about an inch square shone into the room. The door was now permanently locked – there was no way to open it from either side – but at least she could see into the office.

The strip light was on. There was too much furniture in all the wrong places. The main desk was an absolute mess – nothing had changed.

She stood by the window and slid the curtain hooks from the pole. Chuggy's room was above. He was probably the least scary of the men. She found herself looking at the mug Tim had given her, which was still on the bedside table, three quarters of the cocoa still there. Lou sniffed it, put her finger in, licked. It tasted of chocolate.

She returned to the task at hand – trying to get Chuggy's attention. He probably wouldn't hear her as he often had his headphones on. And if he did, he wouldn't be able to do much. It'd take him an hour to get out of bed and into his chair and into the stair lift. And then what?

He might at least call the police, or alert Lunchbox or Tim. Please, Tim. She banged at the ceiling with the pole. Dry plaster fell on her, then some more.

Outside, someone was walking by. Lou shook off the larger lumps of plaster and banged on the window. It was an angel, a woman. She was on stilts and had gigantic, bright wings. Lou knocked and knocked on the glass. The angel smiled back at this fellow artist who was covered in colour and plaster dust. Lou shook her arms – *No, No* – but it was no use, the angel had flown.

The only paper in the room was an old social-work newsletter. She wrote in the only pen in the room (green, almost invisible): *HELP, SOMEONE HAS LOCKED ME IN THIS ROOM, PLEASE CALL 999!* Using some old Blu-tack from the wall she stuck the note to the window.

Footsteps. She ran to the door and looked out the hole. No-one was there yet. The door from the office to the hall was still closed. She couldn't hear footsteps anymore, only her heart. She was breathing too fast. She slid to the floor and put her head between her knees. If only she could go back – *I'm on the bed, I'm watching* I Should be Dead – if only she did *not* fall asleep. If she had stayed awake she would not be trembling on the floor of a small, dark room in a house with a bunch of nutjobs. She knew what MAPPA levels two and three meant now – she'd looked it up. It meant dangerous. This might not be a practical joke or a friendly robbery. She might be in trouble.

The single bed had drawers underneath it that were jam-packed with books or something. The weight made it harder to drag across the room, but it was a more stable barricade once she managed. If someone scary tried to get in, it'd be harder for them at least.

Lou filled the kettle, switched it on, and put everything useful on the carpet tiles in front of the bed – one broken, jagged knife, one mug, one curtain pole, curtain ties, bleach and Fairy Liquid. She crouched on the bed, her hand protected by a bloody tea towel, and held the knife, her eye steady at the hole.

She waited.

And reboiled the kettle.

And sharpened her blade using the rough bottom of the mug.

And waited.

She could hear singing a street or so away. She raced to the window but the street was empty. No it wasn't. A dark figure with several large bags was walking her way. He had a hoodie on. He was turning into this house, head down, fumbling with keys.

She followed the rattle of the keys into the hallway, her knife shaking as she held it in position at the hole in the door, watching to see who was going to come into the office.

The hooded man kicked the door shut and put his Tesco bags on the desk. He had his back to her. She couldn't see his face. He took a bottle of whisky out of one of the bags, opened it, had a skull. 'What the fuck?' he said, seeing the hole in the door and the handle on the floor. He walked towards her, with his head down, whisky bottle in hand.

She could see the handle of a knife in his back pocket as he bent down. When his eye met Lou's, he jumped.

It was Doug. She took a breath, she could relax. Just Doug.

'Fuck's sake,' he said, 'you scared the shite out of me.'

CHAPTER NINETEEN

Doug sat at the desk, took a fist-sized bag of white powder from his pocket, prepared it, snorted it, rubbed his gums with it, ahhhed.

'I'm not gonna hurt you,' he said. 'You have nothing to worry about.'

'Then why am I locked in here and why do you have a knife?'

He snorted another line, played with his nostrils for a while and skulled some more whisky. He took the large knife from his back pocket, held it in his hand and propelled the office chair with his feet. She dropped her own pathetic weapon and froze as the armed robber rolled towards her, only stopping when his knife almost hit the door. He laughed, steadied himself and moved his mouth towards the hole, as if he was about to say something important. Instead, he blew in her eye.

'The blade's to scare you with,' he said.

Lou screamed. 'HELP, HELP, HELP, TIM, TIM, CHUGGY, CHUGGY, HELP ME.' She thumped at the door and at the window with her fists. She kicked at the walls. She prodded the ceiling with the curtain pole, hit the pole against the door and mini fridge. She screamed and yelled and threw things around the room until she was out of breath.

Silence. There was no movement in Chuggy's room above, no footsteps downstairs, no sound in the house at all. No-one was coming to help her.

'They're all out for the count,' Doug said, 'after a nice cup of hot chocolate. Most of them have headphones on too. We all hate hearing each other at night. So you can make a noise. Shout. And while you're doing that I'll go to your flat and talk to your best pal, Becks. She's pretty – famous too. I bet she's got lots of money.'

Doug held her flat keys to the hole, jiggled them. She went boiling hot with the possibility that he might let himself into the flat and join the party and no-one would notice. Or, if they were all asleep, he might creep about, take wallets and phones and the petty cash from Becks's play. He might wake up the old lady in the lounge and make her have a heart attack. Cam might intervene and get killed. Becks might try and stab him with a kitchen knife and do it wrong and die. This harmless, paranoid drug dealer was off his face. He was desperate. He was armed with a knife.

Lou remembered her dad's advice: *You can make a weapon out of almost anything.* Out of sight by the window, Lou lay the curtain pole on the floor, placed the handle of the knife in the hollow of one end, and stood on the malleable metal until it flattened around the handle.

'That's better, thanks,' Doug said. 'I hate shouting, any conflict, because of my childhood. I've been dying to tell you my plan.' He twirled his chair and took a long glug of whisky, bought on her Visa card, probably.

Lou was busy on the floor, keeping as quiet as she could while she peeled a section of curtain tie and twirled the string around the joint between pole and blade. There, the blade was firmly set within its makeshift four-foot handle.

'How much did you spend?' she asked, testing the strength of the joint by prodding at the floor. It was firm, perfect. It was a spear. She was beginning to feel angry that he was spending her money. She wouldn't be paid for another month, had spent most of her money with (or on) Tim, and needed to find somewhere to live. The cocaine must have cost Doug a few hundred pounds, and the Tesco bags were filled with large bottles of spirits. She only had three thousand pounds left in her account, for rent, for life. Alan wasn't putting $8000 in each month anymore, he wasn't paying for the flat, for her bills, her nail technician, dinners out, all those online courses she half did.

Lou crouched on the bed, head low, and placed the point of her spear just underneath the hole. If he tried to hurt her – or Becks – she would jab him.

'I bought booze at three different supermarkets,' Doug said, 'organised swapsies with my pal for this beauty.' He wiggled his bag of powder, then prepared and snorted another line. 'Woohoo! Do you only have the Visa?'

'Yes. What's your plan, Doug?' She loosened her grip on the pole; couldn't imagine jabbing him. Jabbing was stabbing.

'I am dying to tell you the plan. You're not gonna believe it.'

'What is it?'

His facial features were veering off in different directions. He took another snort, another glug. 'You have two hours to get five grand. I transfer the money from your account to theirs, which is Swiss or crypto, or some fucking bollocks. I've promised it'll be in the account at 4am, which means there is a ticking time bomb in this situation. We have one hour and fifty-nine minutes to pay up, or they come and get me. We really do need to work together and move this forward.'

'Come on, why would they kill you for five grand? You said they're great guys. They're dads aren't they?'

'They get the job done when it has to be done. They'd kill for a tenner.' He picked up his knife in an attempt to be threatening. 'So would I.'

It'd be best to find the money, she decided. She wouldn't get credit online – poor employment history, no credit rating. And she couldn't think of anyone with spare cash. Mostly she couldn't think of anyone she was close enough to ask.

Doug had taken a moment to refill his nostril and gob, and was now back on the plan. He rolled his chair to the door and twirled from side to side in excitement. 'When I've paid them, I go hand myself in down the road and the cops come save you. And this is the best bit: you claim the money back on insurance or compensation or something, or even both, so you're not out of pocket – better off even – and you're a poor victim and a major hero. Everyone's gonna love you. Meanwhile…' snort, glug '…I'm safe inside and I don't owe any crazy grieving sons any fucking thing … Good plan huh?'

'It's an excellent plan, except that I don't have five thousand pounds. I have – had – three thousand on my Visa card.'

'Three grand, excellent, I only spent a few hundred.'

He went frantic on his phone, holding up her Visa card to transcribe the numbers. It was making her angry.

'I'm doing some shopping,' he said. The drugs and the alcohol were really kicking in now. He was forgetting the plan.

'Doug, no. Hang on. I've still got two thousand, seven hundred in my account, right. So if I transfer that to you, we just need to find two thousand, three hundred. That won't be hard. Do you have some stolen phones you can sell? Maybe I could get an overdraft online? Let's work this out together. I won't tell anyone.'

It was too late. Doug was in shopping ecstasy. He was

holding up Lou's Visa card again. 'Ya beauty,' he said. 'Chanel number nine, Carrie-Annie's favourite, to be delivered to…' He was typing in the order.

'I thought she was sleeping with her ex-stepfather.'

'Yeah, yeah, but she'll want me when I'm inside. Women love locked-up bad-boys, weak and desperate and full of romantic dreams and promises they intend to keep. You can claim this. You can say I took some expensive jewellery as well, if you know what I mean, like a watch or a ring or a bracelet. This is gonna work out really well for you.' His pupils were all over the place. 'So if you were buying a chaise sofa for your ma, would you buy it in green velvet or in blue velvet?' He held up his phone so she could see the sofas, but she refused to answer. He went for the green, to be delivered to his ma's homeless hostel within five to eight weeks.

'Fuck!' Doug thought it had said 'days'. 'Too late,' he said. 'Anyway, I'm pretty certain she'll still be there.' He bought a fish tank plus fish paraphernalia, as well as several tropical fish, to be delivered to his aunty Margaret's. He bought a gaming monitor, to be delivered to his pal Mince and a burner phone for him to smuggle in on a visit.

Lou closed her eyes and tried to relax. She imagined she was on a beach in Greece, and not in this place. Greece – she could go there next, get a job in a bar, meet a fun BF.

She could work part time in a warm colourful beach bar. There'd be sunshine and seafood…

Doug turned up Dolly Parton on his phone. 'We've got to get on this,' he said. 'Let's get going.' He started dancing, had some nifty moves. 'This is not a relapse, Lou. This is not even a lapse. This is my last hurrah. You getting me – you getting it? I love it. I fucking love it. *I will always love you*…' He fell back onto the chair.

Greece had faded. Lou was now seething on the floor, sharpening her blade on the bottom of the mug.

When his shopping spree was finally over, Doug took a breath and looked through the hole. 'Hey, where are you?'

Lou popped up from the floor, sat on the bed.

'I'm really not gonna hurt you. I like you. I appreciate how you listened to me. You seemed to at least try to care, like upstairs, y'know, when you were asking about family. Do you think your mum and dad would help us out?'

'They don't have any money,' Lou said. In reality, her mother had a savings account that she put her hairdressing money into each month. It was her personal stash from the jobs she had, on and off. Her dad always lived from payday to payday, spent all his money on family life and fishing. He believed in living, not saving.

'I'm gonna ask your mum and dad,' Doug said. 'I just need your passcode.'

She was about to say it out loud, get this over with, but

she could not remember it. She'd never used the code, always the thumb. And it had been two years since Becks set it up for her. They were drying toenail polish on the balcony in Port Melbourne, sipping margheritas.

'Six digits,' Doug said. 'What are they?'

It was a date, it was a birthday. That's right, it was Becks's birthday. When was that?

She should know it. Becks shoved it down her throat every year, had a themed party that Lou sometimes couldn't get out of. 'I can't remember, honestly.'

'Bullshit.'

'It's something like 560876,' Lou lied. It was nothing like that. She knew most of it. Born in 1999. But what day in December? That was the problem with Becks's birthday. December. Even if it was on the first of December, which Lou didn't think it was – hang on, it might be – it was still awfully close to Christmas. No-one should be expected to remember a December birthday.

'Try 560877,' she said to Doug.

He typed it in. 'Stop fucking pissing me about.' He threw something at the door, it smashed. He punched the door at shoulder height, made a tiny crack in it.

'Just use my thumb,' Lou said, poking it through the hole.

Doug sat back in his chair and swivelled as he compiled his masterpiece on the unlocked phone, asking for notes from Lou along the way.

Hi Mum and Dad,

I'm doing okay but I'm afraid I'm needing some cash urgently. I've completely run out of money. I have an amazing job with SASOL, loving it. I feel I am really helping people. The problem is that my first pay won't come in for another month and I owe the deposit and the rent for the flat with Becks (we are having so much fun together). I also need a little bit for food and bills. Would it be possible to borrow £5,000? I can pay you it all back within two months. I'm afraid I have some work to do in relation to budgeting.

Love you both,

Lou xx

PS: If you are able to lend me the money, can you please do an immediate transfer to my Visa?

Doug was very careful to include the correct bank details. He pressed send, then started going through her phone.

'What are you doing with Tim anyway?' he said, obviously reading her messages. 'Haven't you Googled him? I'm sorry, I should have warned you.'

'Yeah, the hostage-taker with the knife should have warned me … Did you know about me before I started work? Did Tim tell you about us?'

'How could I have known you? What do you mean? Were you with Tim before you started the job? Holy shit.

Holy shit! You are fucking naughty.' He kept flicking through her phone. 'Oh Lou. Oh, no, no, Lou.' He was zooming in on something. 'Tit pic, really?'

'Please don't share that,' she said.

'Oh my god, is that a snuff movie, oh thank god, it's you. No no no no no Lou. Oh, Lou.'

She should have taken Tim's advice and deleted all that. Idiot. 'Please, please, my mum and dad would get really upset.'

'Oh god, I would never,' Doug said. 'My wee cousin had that done to her, by an ex, the revenge porn, she ended up playing chicken on the M6.'

'Is she okay?'

'It was the M6. I would never do that to you. I don't want to hurt you. I really don't. I would never ever—'

The phone made him jump. It was her mum.

'Just confirm what you've said,' Doug said, holding the phone to the hole. 'Say you need it NOW and nothing else, please. Answer.'

'Mum,' Lou said through the hole, her heart melting. If only she could sob and say: *Help me. Mum, help me.*

'Lou,' her mother's voice was calm, loving. 'Are you okay? What time is it there?'

Lou's lips were shaking. It was hard to sound normal. 'I'm good, it's beautiful here. It's the middle of the night.'

'Did the jacket arrive yet?'

'Not yet. Thanks though.'

'I should have paid the extra,' her mum said.

'Becks and I are loving the jam, it's like toast with butter and home. Mum, I'm sorry about everything, with Alan and all that, the things I said.'

'It's okay, baby girl. Dad's saying don't be daft, it's all good. You sound sad. Come home.'

Doug was making a throat-slitting gesture. She should get a move on.

'I'm great, I am. Sorry, a bit homesick. I'm at work, it's the middle of the night, and I need the rent and deposit. It's really expensive here. Sorry to ask.'

'Don't be, budgeting is hard. I'm so proud of what you're doing. Sure you're okay, though, you sound strange?'

Lou was no longer able to sound normal. She was crying.

'My darling, what's wrong?'

'Nothing, nothing. I miss you. And I'm sorry, about everything. Tell Dad I love him.'

'Dad's saying he loves you too. And that he's put some shelves up in your room.'

'My room?'

'You always have a room here.'

That was true, wherever *here* was, there was always a bedroom, set up just how she liked it: her childhood map-top desk under the window, bed with floral duvet cover against the wall. Her dad always put up shelves for her collection of snow globes from the many snowless places she had lived; her survival books; her fossils; and her favourite photos (camping with Dad, having her hair done by Mum).

'I'll put that money in now, my darling,' her mum said. 'And don't worry about paying it back. We can sort that out later.'

'Thank you,' Lou said.

'Wind it up,' Doug mouthed from the other side of the door.

'I've got to go, I love you.'

Doug hung up, grinned. 'I love your mum, she sounds really kind. You will remember to claim for this and pay her back? Promise? Could you give her a bit extra if you get enough?'

Lou rolled her eyes. 'I promise.'

He put Lou's phone on the office desk and snorted a thick line of powder. He circled the desk, making calls on his own phone. Lou was starting to worry – or hope – that he might overdose. He could hardly stand up, and his voice was slurry but fast and filled with passion:

'Jimbo! I know, I'm sorry, it's just I'm going back in, wanted to say ciao … No, it's good, it's what I want. It's fucking brutal out here. Everyone I know can only do this unconscious. Will you visit me? Send me some money on my birthday or whenever? … Okay, I know, sorry, get some sleep now … See ya, pal.'

'Sam? I'll have it in the account any moment. It's sorted.'

'Ma! … I know what time it is – Ma? Guess what I bought … Ma?'

He stopped at the desk, checked Lou's phone. The screen had gone blank. 'I need your thumb again.'

'It lights up if a message comes through,' Lou said.

'Then it fades. Give me your thumb.' He walked over and held the screen at the hole.

She did as she was told but it was really starting to piss her off.

'She hasn't paid up,' he said, having checked Lou's messages.

His tone and his face were changing. He could kill her, she realised. He could knock down the door and kill her.

'Sam?' Doug's face was white. 'Oh, hi, Tony, sorry for the delay, won't be long.' He hung up and typed something into Lou's phone. 'I've texted your friend Becks,' he said, putting her phone back on the office desk. 'She has twenty minutes to put the money in or I'm going over there.' He took another line of coke.

Lou had blocked Becks, which meant she wouldn't get the message. She couldn't decide if this was good or bad.

He circled the desk again, leaving messages:

'Carrie-Annie, it's Doug, I'm just ringing to say…' He

started sobbing, hung up, dialled another number immediately, face tight this time: 'If you go near my girlfriend again I will kill you and your family, you fucking paedo.' Doug punched the desk, making a small cocaine cloud. He began pacing the room, his sobbing more dramatic each circuit. He opened the office door an inch and kept peering into the hall. Occasionally, he punched a wall. His knuckles were bleeding.

Her dad's advice: *Never lose focus.* She steadied herself on the carpet, spear in hand, blade poised at the bottom of the fortress hole.

When her phone beeped on the desk and the screen lit up, Doug raced over and picked it up, reading part of the message before it faded. 'Your mum,' he said. 'I need your thumb again.'

'Nup,' she said. 'Fuck off.'

He began kicking at the bottom of the door, but got nowhere, thanks to her bed-barricade. He punched the door at shoulder height, over and over until it cracked again, leaving his hand cut and bleeding. With the knife, he stabbed and stabbed at the crack he'd made in the door, until the point of his blade came through to her side. If he kept going, he would get in.

Lou wriggled into the perfect position and tightened her grip. She lifted the blade into the centre of the hole. It was shaking. She breathed, steadied it. In only sixty minutes or so, this absolute knob had taken Lou hostage, scared her to death, stolen all her money, taken her mother's savings and threatened her best friend. Imagine what he could do with the rest of the cocaine, the rest of the whisky, another sixty minutes.

He was standing on the other side of the door now, knife in hand. He held up the screen of her phone. 'Thumb or I'll fucking kill you.'

She jabbed her spear forward a little, knocking the phone from Doug's hand and poking him in the hip.

He let out a yelp, grabbed at the rip in his jeans. 'There's blood. What the fuck?' he said, bending down to look in the hole.

Lou might have roared as she thrust the spear.

CHAPTER TWENTY

She wasn't sure what just happened. She was still holding the curtain pole. But it was a foot shorter than it was before. She loosened her grip, let go. It remained exactly where it was, almost straight, hip height, levitating, steady in the air. She flicked the pole with the back of her hand. It didn't move. One quarter of her spear was firmly stuck in something on the other side of the door. Her feet were frozen on the carpet. 'Doug?'

Silence.

'Doug?' Oh god, Doug. She was too scared to look up close; did not want to know what her spear was stuck in. 'Doug, Doug, say something, say something, I'm sorry, I'm so sorry.' She started trembling violently, crying. But this was no time for hysterics, no time to shake and bawl. She breathed in, out, composed herself.

'Doug! Someone?'

Nothing.

She moved closer to the hole. The pole was taking up most of the space, but not all of it. She didn't understand why she could only see blackness around its round edges. She took hold of the spear, used both hands to move it half a centimetre to one side. Her eye was as close as it could get. She could see … it was hard to tell. What was that?

She changed tack, decided to push the pole and move the obstruction away from the door. It was too heavy, it would not budge. She was thinking of the obstruction as 'it'. It might not be Doug. It might be the chair. Or something. Not Doug. Please, not Doug.

She pulled at the pole but it was a heavy snag. She pulled again – *Bring it in Louie, all your might. Focus…* Nothing happened but the slightest of sucking noises that made her throw up in the sink and start crying again.

Stupid, stupid girl. She jumped on the bed and had a proper look this time, her eye directly beside the pole, directly above, directly opposite…

…an eyebrow.

She screamed. She was looking at Doug's eyebrow. The blade had gone in through his eye socket. One quarter of her spear – about one foot – was inside his head. The blade must have lodged itself in the back of his skull.

She yelled, prodded the crumbling ceiling, banged on the window, banged on the sink, smashed a mug, kicked the fridge. Someone was walking down the street, a very drunk older man, staggering not walking, head down, bottle in hand. She managed to stand on the windowsill, arms outstretched, her pale-green *SOS* note on the glass between her legs. Surely he would see her. He did. He was looking at her.

And now he wasn't. Now he was staggering across the road and peeing in Posh Pastel's front courtyard.

Please, Posh Pastel, please open your curtains and look outside.

She thought about taking her top off. Someone would notice her then. Although no-one seemed to notice when Rob wanked in the window below.

A noise in the hall. Footsteps. Someone had heard her, at last. She jumped down from the sill. 'Hello? Help! Someone? Tim, is that you?' She could hear the office door creaking. 'Who's there?' she said. 'Tim? Hello, who is it? Call the police. Please help. Please call 999.'

A man's voice: 'Doug, is that you?'

It was Rob. He was walking towards her, towards Doug. He still hadn't seen the spear.

'Rob, thank god it's you,' she said. 'Thank god.'

'Headlights? What are you doing in there?'

'I'm locked in. I need help.'

'Doug?' he said, standing behind Doug. 'What are you looking at down there? Is this a peephole situation? Are you starkers in there, Headlights?'

'Is he okay?' Lou asked.

'Doug?' Rob patted his room-mate on the shoulder. 'What are you doing, kneeling? Are you praying or something? Doug, hey, Doug?' Suddenly Rob let out a yell: 'FUUUUCK, fucking hell, fuck fuck!' He obviously had the full picture now. 'What is this? Oh my god, what the fuck have you done?'

What had *she* done? 'Is he alive?'

'He's got a fucking pole in his head. Holy shit, holy shit, Doug.' He leaned down as if to hug his dead room-mate, then thought better of it: 'Fuck, DNA, I cannot touch anything. Shite. Fucking shite, fucking bitch, you murdered him. He's dead. Doug's dead, you fucking murdered him.'

'It was pretty obviously a defensive move,' Lou said from the other side of the door. 'He's not breathing?'

'Of course he's fucking not.'

'Call the ambulance, please, call the police. I've been locked in here for ages.'

Rob moved into the middle of the room and put his hands in the air, then realised: 'Fuck, I touched him on the shoulder. Oh no. Fuck, shit, I touched the door handle when I came in. Stacey's gonna murder me. Three days, just three more days to go. I guess if it comes to it, I could say the DNA must have transferred earlier, when he brought me supper, like. He's probably got everyone's DNA on him, right?'

Rob was talking to himself, didn't require an answer.

He wiped the office door handles with his sleeve, scoured the room for any other traces that he may have left behind. He hovered over the desk for a while, littered as it was with Lou's iPhone, lines of cocaine, bottles of whisky. 'No, no, no,' he said. 'You're not gonna tempt me. I am not touching anything.' Hands up, he made his way to the centre of the office again. She could almost hear his brain trying to turn this to his advantage. 'If you tell the cops anything about me, you'll regret it,' he said. 'You did not see me in the basement last night. I'm not here tonight either. Am I here?'

'You're not here,' Lou said. She sat on the bed but really wanted to lie down. She was so tired.

'You say a thing and I'll tell them you're sleeping with the lifer. I heard you two the other night, in the box room. Well I heard him. You were very quiet.' He made a sex sound: 'Ah, ah, ah.'

'I don't care,' Lou said. She really didn't.

'I'll tell them you charge in here for blow jobs.'

'Cool.'

'Twenty quid – we get our money back if you don't swallow.'

Oh Jeez, did this man ever stop being a sex offender? Even with a gruesome body in the room he could get aroused. It was dawning on her that she was under the absolute control of a very-high-risk sex offender. She'd never been scared of him, but she should have been. She should have been scared of all of them. Rob didn't just get his dick out all over the country and wobble it about – *Ooh, look here, looky what I've got* – he followed women on buses and he took opportunities in basements. He sexually assaulted someone once. She should have looked into that. Actually, Polly should have told her what she needed to know about him. For example, that when Rob masturbated about town he wasn't thinking nice things, he was thinking: *Fucking bitch, take it, take it, you fucking whore, I'm gonna get you, I'm gonna fucking get you.*

He looked like he was thinking that now.

'If I let you out will you suck my dick?'

'No.'

'I'll tell them you've got it in for me – and my wife.'

'Go for it. Tell them whatever you like, I don't care. For fuck's sake, Rob, can you not see that I've been taken hostage. Doug's been harassing my family for money. He was breaking the door. Look – he did a Jack Nicholson with his knife.'

'So he did,' Rob said, the knife now in his hand. 'Shite.' He dropped it again, wiped it, put his hands back in the air. He could not trust himself.

'Please ring the police, or go get Tim,' she yelled at him. 'Just fucking ring them.' But there was no negotiating with this sasol. 'TIM!' she screamed. 'TIM!! HELP ME, SOMEBODY HELP ME.'

Rob rushed over to the office door, covered his hand with his T-shirt, closed it. 'Shut the fuck up,' he said.

'You're really not going to ring the police?'

'No.'

'Please, Rob. Please help me. I won't tell them about you in the basement and on the buses in Livingston. If you just dial 999. I'll tell them you came down and saved me. You'll be a hero.'

'Hero.' He laughed. 'Let me tell you how it'll go if I ring 999.' He put a pretend phone to his ear: '"Hiya! It's Robert McKenzie here. I'm a registered sex offender on non-parole licence living in SASOL … Yeah, yeah, *that* place. I'm calling because there's been a hostage situation and a murder…" They wouldn't listen after that. Sirens would start almost straight away. We'd be surrounded. I'd be arrested. You'd be the hero.'

He made his way to the desk, put his hands behind his back, careful not to touch anything. He then lowered his head a few centimetres above the cocaine and sniffed. 'Fuck that!' he said, moving back into his safe position. 'I won't end up charged with some fucking thing because of the mess you made. Fucking shoulder, why did I touch him, why did I touch the door? FUCK THIS. Three more days. I am not standing here. I did not come down to this office. I did not touch anything. I was – *am* – upstairs in bed.'

'Okay,' Lou said. She'd given up on getting Rob's help and was now putting her efforts into not getting raped. 'I won't say anything. You weren't in the basement, you're not here. I promise.'

He started wiping the door handles with his sleeve again. 'I am going up to my bed. I'm going to shut the door, put my headphones on and sleep. I know nothing.'

He was about to leave when Lou's phone beeped on the desk. Rob pounced over and read the message out loud before the screen faded. '*5K in your account. Love you…* Who's that from?' he asked.

'It's from my mum. Doug made me get it out of her. It was for his debt.'

'Is it five thousand dollars or five thousand pounds?'

'None of your business … Pounds.'

'Give it to me and I'll help you.' He held her phone up to the crack in the door, which was at head height. The crack was long and thin and jagged, but there was one space wide enough for a thumb. 'Need your thumb for the transfer.'

'And then you'll call the police, yes?'

'Pinky promise,' he said.

She poked her thumb out, almost got a splinter on the way back. Ouch.

'Ta … Five thousand pounds! I'm gonna take Trace to the Crieff Hydro.' He celebrated his windfall by hoovering more cocaine. 'What are you wearing by the way?'

'Can you call 999 now, please?' She held her knees to her chest and said a prayer: 'Dear God, please make him call the police, please don't let him in, please don't let him get me.'

'Who are you talking to?' someone said. A man. It wasn't Rob.

Oh, thank god. She knelt on the bed, peeked through the crack. It was Tim.

CHAPTER TWENTY-ONE

Tim was here to save her, at last. He'd only noticed Rob so far, though. 'What are you doing?' he said.

Rob was hoovering white powder from the desk with a huge grin on his face.

'Is that cocaine?'

'"Is that cocaine?"' Rob mimicked Tim's accent. He had nothing to add. He was celebrating.

Tim still hadn't noticed the dead man in the room. 'Tim, it's me. I'm in here,' she said through the crack in the door.

'Lou? What are you doing in there? Did you lock her in there, Rob? Did you fucking hurt her? I will kill you.' Tim grabbed him by the pyjama top. Lou was glad that Rob was too off his face to notice.

'Did I hurt *her*?' he laughed.

'He didn't hurt me,' Lou said through the crack.

'Look over there. No, look down, dickhead,' Rob said. 'She killed Doug. Look.' He pointed.

Tim let go of Rob, walked over to the slumped man and tapped him on the shoulder. 'Doug? Doug? Hey, Doug? Oh no, oh my god. Oh my god.'

'She's a crazy fucking psycho,' Rob said, taking another snort of cocaine then rubbing his nose long and hard.

'Lou? Are you okay?' Tim said through the crack.

'Just a small cut on my hand, I'm fine.'

'What happened? Holy shit, how did you do that? Oh my god.'

'He locked me in when I was asleep, robbed me, got off his face, went nuts. I think he drugged everyone's hot chocolate. Are the other two awake yet?'

'Don't think so. Let me get you out,' he said. 'It went … Wow, it went straight through his eye. What did you make this thing with?'

'Curtain pole, butter knife, string.'

'Stand back from the door and I'll give it a kick.'

'You shouldn't touch anything,' Rob said, body swaying, jaw clenched, face grey. 'This is a crime scene.'

'He's right,' Lou said. 'Don't get me out, don't touch anything, just call the police.'

'Okay,' Tim said, taking out his phone. 'No more of that cocaine,' he said to Rob, who was leaning over the desk again. 'You can hardly stand up and you're leaving snot everywhere. Don't touch anything, Rob. Not a thing. All that happened is you heard Lou yell, came down, found this. It's the truth. Nothing to do with us, long as we don't touch a thing.'

'I'm not touching anything,' Rob said. 'See, there's just the air between my nostrils and the desk.' He sniffed again, confident of no transference, then leaned over the arm of the sofa and dry-retched loudly. He composed himself, phew. Then he did it again.

This happened five times, each so vivid and contagious that Lou ended up doing it too.

'Phew,' Rob said, swallowing. 'That was close.' Then he leaned over and puked large chunks onto the carpet tiles.

'Fuck, mate, you're whiteying big time,' Tim said.

Rob had a big stomach with a lot in it, once. 'Oh god, oh god, where's the loo? It's coming out the other end…' He puked, then sat on his heel to stop it happening at the other end. 'It's coming, it's…'

Rob's face said it all.

'Oh god, no,' Tim said as the deluge continued, loudly. 'The cops can't see him like this. I'll clean him up in the downstairs loo, change his clothes, then I'll call 999. Is that okay?'

'Okay,' she said. 'Two minutes.'

Rob let loose again. His pants were changing colour.

Tim put his pinky through the crack in the door (it was the only finger that would fit) and touched hers. 'I'll fix him up then I'll get you out of here. You sure you'll be all right? I'll be as fast as I can. You're safest in there, I think, don't you?'

She agreed. She lay on the bed, closed her eyes and counted in her head: *One-cat-dog, two-cat-dog, three-cat-dog.* She was breathing normally for the first time in hours. The kettle was not boiling; no need to turn it on again. She would walk out of this building unharmed, perhaps even a hero like Doug said.

PRESENTER: When a young night worker is taken hostage in a halfway house, the affluent residents of the gothic new town of Edin-borough, Scotland, are angry and they are battening down the hatches.

Posh Pastel: This cannot go on. Thugs and paedophiles do not belong in Nevis Place.
Neighbour: I have to admit Doug was the kind of guy to get murdered.

'Murdered', is that what they'd call it?

PRESENTER: But no-one has anything bad to say about Lou O'Dowd.

Neil, Project Worker, SASOL: She's lovely.
Cam from Canberra: I really liked her shoe system.
Gregor from the Plane: Best long-haul drinking buddy I've ever had.

Lou had lost count. Perhaps she was at about fifteen-cat-dog. She resumed: *Sixteen-cat-dog, seventeen-cat-dog…*

She wished she hadn't puked and peed in the sink earlier, it was blocked, did not drain well. Tim and the cops would think she was gross.

She also wished she hadn't killed Doug.

She took that back. She was glad to have killed Doug. It was him or her. The stuff of the battlefield.

She would breathe fresh air soon – any second – and go home to her pillow. She would cry for a while and sleep for days.

Sirens, soon she would hear sirens.

Two minutes must have been up by now. She knelt to check on the office door – no sign of Tim and Rob but she could hear them talking. It sounded like they were in the kitchen.

She was safe in this room. This would be over any minute. With the broken piece of blade, she scraped out *Lou was here 2023* on the skirting board where the bed was. She wondered if she should move the bed back to its original position, so she could get out more easily when the police came. It was so heavy, though. She was too tired to drag it back. She scolded herself for not having checked the drawers under the bed sooner. Perhaps there was something useful there, like a fully charged phone or a gun or a Mars bar.

There were two large drawers under the bed. In one there were six plastic boxes, each with a lid, each with the name of a resident on the top. She opened Chuggy's: half a bottle of vodka, a packet of Marlboro cigarettes and a smelly suit – for court appearances, she supposed. She realised she was cold and put on the blue polyester jacket.

Tim's box contained dozens of letters addressed to him at HMP Edinburgh. Fan mail, some including photos of the many young beautiful women who believed in Tim:

I love you Tim. That last visit was magic. In support of your campaign for a pardon, I am sending you £20, £30, £40; and, in one case, *£300.* There were betting slips, his winning ones, she supposed, happy memories. There were five Gucci shirts, tags on, a shiny pair of brogues, a gorgeous French-looking vase, a Rolex in its box, and a gold cross on a chain, also in its box.

The other drawer was chock-a-block with loose files and reports. This must be Polly's secret filing cabinet. She didn't even keep it locked, just positioned the bed so the drawers were against the wall. The drawer was stuffed with pre-release reports, pre-sentence reports, child-protection reports, lists of criminal convictions and worksheets regarding offending behaviour. That's right, Polly liked to have collateral.

Lou flicked through some of the pages:

There were hundreds of hand-written incident forms: 'Worker followed home', 'Lunchbox suicidal' (there were about a hundred of these). 'Worker threatened on Facebook', 'Worker assaulted'. The latter was written by Jacky from the borders:

It was a cold morning. Nevis Place was strewn with litter from the night before. I heard a knock on the door.

Jacky must be writing a novel, bless her. Lou did not have time to read it.

Maybe she should yell – *Tim, what's happening?* She'd have to yell for him to hear her from the kitchen. She'd wake the others up. Or perhaps time was going more slowly than she thought. Two minutes was never going to be enough time to sort Rob out. Tim probably had to put him in the shower, get clothes from upstairs, put a load of washing on. She'd be patient, breathe, distract herself.

Lou found herself shaking the French vase in Tim's box: empty. She opened the Rolex box. The watch said 9am. Must need a battery. She touched the velvet padding, then pulled it all out, unsure what she was looking for. There was nothing behind the velvet. She put the watch back in its box and returned her attention to the paperwork.

So this was where incident forms went to die, no action taken. Lou started reading Neil's 'Worker threatened with chair' report:

Rob came into the office at 6.30pm. He was clearly agitated and stated: 'I'm not going to that fucking paedo ring.' He was referring to the sex offender's group-work programme, which he is required to attend by law. 'They give me the colouring-in every time,' Rob said. He was referring to the warm-up exercises given to the group members, which consists of three options: mindfulness, colouring-in, or a fidget spinner. Rob then picked up an office chair and threatened to throw it at the writer if I didn't ring ahead to demand he get the fidget spinner. 'Let the paedos do the colouring in,' he said. The writer managed to calm Rob down with a cigarette and he left for the group ten minutes late. NB: the writer has had feedback from one of the group workers that Rob is 'too lazy to colour in'.

There was a pre-release report regarding Peter Cowey, more widely known as Lunchbox, who had raped an eleven-year-old girl backstage in Berlin, a fourteen-year-old girl in his trailer on Loch Lomond, and a twelve-year-old girl in a hotel room in Kensington. In the 'Accommodation' section of the report, it was noted that Mr Cowey had been moved seven times since his release. Bricks had been thrown through his windows in Glasgow, Aberdeen and Dundee; protestors had made life impossible in Helensburgh and even Portree. SASOL was the only place that would take him in.

She put her ear to the crack in the door. She could hear the men talking, still in the downstairs kitchen by the sounds. They might have already called the police.

In the drawer there was the indictment for Robert McKenzie, AKA Rob, who had grabbed a woman outside a bar in the city centre of Glasgow, held her by the throat against the bin, ripped off her pants, and penetrated her vagina roughly with his fingers, to her injury.

She was getting annoyed, and scared. Tim was taking too long. She wanted to yell for him but decided, once again, that he was probably being as fast as possible. She would be safe for another two minutes.

In the drawer there was a pre-sentence report for Charles (Chuggy) Garvery, who had spent four hours on the phone to nineteen-year-old Gail Benson before she jumped off a bridge. 'You can do it', he kept saying to the victim. 'You are strong enough to do this. Just take one step, just one step'.

She found a letter to Chuggy from his wife Deirdre. 'I never want to see you again', she wrote. 'If you ever try to contact me, I'll tell them what you've actually been talking to Ben about, and how you're planning to film it. I'll tell them about *Vrie*'.

WTF was *Vrie*? Looked like a link. Chuggy probably had another dark website going.

'I hope you rot in hell', his wife signed off.

Lou hoped he did too.

She could hear the men talking a little more loudly now. It sounded like two voices still, no more. Thank god Lunchbox and Chuggy were still upstairs. The last thing she needed was for those two to enter the equation.

In the drawer there was a psychiatric assessment for Douglas Wilson that concluded he wasn't insane, and listed, in stark bullet-point form, the never-ending tragedies that had befallen him, one terrible thing after another: his father a killer, his mother so ill, his sister dead, his brother dead, everyone dying in godawful ways. Doug.

Lou put her hand to the door and sobbed. She imagined Doug's mother finding out about this. She could see her, sitting on an enormous green-velvet sofa, saying: 'This arrived six weeks after he died, like a sign.'

Lou couldn't stop crying. 'I'm so sorry, Doug.'

Tim should have come back by now. She could hear the voices – they were louder, happier. Was Tim laughing? All this waiting was starting to piss her off.

She sifted through the reports to find his name. Timothy Wilson – there were no incident reports. He was a model resident. She found a page titled 'Action Plan', factors relevant to his offending in order of importance:

1. Violence
2. Gambling addiction
3. Alcohol and drug (cocaine) use
4. Low self-esteem

Surely violence was not his biggest problem? She imagined what Neil, and even Becks, would say: 'Do not forget he's a double murderer.' Lou had even underlined those words on her pad two nights before. Right enough, she supposed murder would knock low self-esteem from the number one spot.

She found the minutes of a pre-release meeting. In prison, Tim had completed every course going – gambling awareness, alcohol and drugs awareness, anger management, yoga. He was a hard worker. Never violent. Tim was a model prisoner.

On the top of one pile, she found a hand-written exercise. Tim had completed it two days ago.

<u>Write about something bad that happened to you.</u>
I was fifteen. Dad chucked all Ruth's clothes and stuff out on the lawn. She was seventeen and pregnant by an inappropriate local, Lady Chatterley's Lover *kind of thing, only the lover was forty-one. I told Dad to stop it and he punched me and I lost it. Lucky for both of us, I was off to St Andrews the following week. I wish I never headbutted him back. I wish he could have been a kinder person.*

<u>Write about something good that happened to you.</u>
I've met someone. I have never had so much fun – or laughed so much – in my life. I am going to be honest with this girl. I am going to tell her everything, tomorrow. I am taking her to meet Ruth. I never thought I could be happy again. I never thought I deserved it. I really think I am in with a chance of being happy. Happy!

It might have been love she was feeling, it might have been nausea. Unsure, Lou went to splash her face in the sink, but it still hadn't drained. She wanted to vomit. She also needed to pee again. She took her jeans and the polyester jacket off, climbed up onto the sink and squatted. Her flow was angry and some of it splashed right back at her. What a relief, though, even if the sink was never going to drain. There was already a yellow-brick tide mark. Nice.

What was taking him so long? She was starting to think she'd be better off with Lunchbox and/or Chuggy in the equation; that she should yell, scream.

Not yet. She'd give it another minute or two.

She decided to widen the space Doug had made with his knife. If there were any issues when they came back in, she could trick them into passing her phone through, or maybe she could grab it.

She knelt on the bed again, had a peek, and began picking away at the crack with her fingers, pulling away small strips of wood one at a time. Her fingers were getting splintered. But this might work.

The door to the hall was opening. Thank god. Tim was here, Rob freshly dressed and smiling.

'So sorry about that,' Tim said. 'Rob needed a bit of a wash. Also, I doubled your money. You can pay your parents back.'

Rob held up his phone with a huge grin. His account balance was now £9,500.

'I negotiated that we get half,' Tim said. 'Two and a half grand – half what we owe to your folks.'

Sucking blood from her finger, Lou found herself saying 'Thank you.'

'Rob's been trying to convince me to double it again,' Tim said.

Lou had not been asked a question. She said nothing.

'He can double that in thirty seconds,' Rob said. 'You should have seen him go back there.'

'No,' Lou said, 'just call the police.'

'It'd be a relief to pay back the whole five to your parents, plus the two grand I owe,' Tim said.

'Wasn't it seventeen hundred?' Lou said.

'It *was*.'

'Let's just do it,' Rob said. 'It's in my account, on my phone. We don't need her permission.'

Becks had once said: 'If a man tells you who he is, believe him.' Tim had told her he couldn't think about anything else if there was a bet to be had. She should not be shocked to see it in action.

'Just one more minute – could be life-changing.'

Again, he hadn't asked a question. She stared at him. He was starting to look unfamiliar. His face was not so pretty. At the same time, she really did want the whole five grand. It was her mum's hairdressing money. It was hard-earned.

Rob sat on the non-puke section of the sofa. 'What do I get then, if you double it?'

'Ten for me and Lou...'

Me and Lou, aw.

'...Ten for you,' Tim said. 'We could repay your folks with interest, Lou.'

Lou would love to repay her mum with interest.

'Fifty-fifty,' Rob said, hand out to seal the deal.

The men shook hands and Rob handed his phone over.

Tim inhaled like a madman, pushed the chair Doug had once swivelled on and positioned it at the desk. He sat, moved the lever so the chair was lower.

Rob was standing behind him now, vodka bottle in hand, swaying from side to side to ease his nerves. 'Want me to do anything to help?' he asked.

'If you could stand back a bit ... two more inches ... that's it,' Tim said. 'Maybe breathe through your nose, yeah?'

Rob stood in the right place and breathed the right way. Tim worked on getting his chair in the perfect position – one last adjustment, a centimetre higher – and then cracked his knuckles. He blew cocaine dust off the office computer. He placed the phone in the perfect position, and cracked his knuckles again. Finally, he exhaled. He was about to do the most important thing in the world. No-one else could do this, just Tim. The future of human existence was in his hands, or thumbs. 'Righty-oh, here we go, here we go.'

Lou could see Tim's face as he stared at the phone. His eyes were crazy, stressed. She could hear the music of the online casino, the *chucka-chucka-chucka* then the *ping-ping-ping*. Bells to excite your brain, and boy were they dinging with Tim. It was disconcerting, his expression, a mixture of ecstasy and pain – holy shit, it was his orgasm face.

'Done!' he said, showing Rob.

'Twenty grand, oh my god, no way, no way, show me again, twenty thousand pounds.'

Rob's huge hairy face seemed jovial, like someone you might ask for directions. He was so happy he could dance. Some high-fiving and woo-hooing and fuck-me-ing was happening. They now had twenty thousand pounds, ten each.

'I can double that,' Tim said, holding Rob's gaze.

'Yes!' said Rob.

'No, quit!' Lou said. 'Tim, don't bet again, you'll just lose it. If you get into debt Ruth'll know you're gambling. She already suspects you are. You could lose your half of Tavisdale. Time to stop, hey, Tim? Time to call the police?'

It was too late. She had lost the Tim she thought she knew. He had not even heard her.

'I turn this twenty-grand into forty,' Tim said. 'You get twenty, Lou and I get twenty.'

The 'Lou and I', 'me and Lou' thing was starting to grate. Also, this was her mother's money. She should be getting it all. 'Please get a grip, Tim. Stop,' Lou said.

But he was shaking hands with Rob and making his way into position at the desk. Rob began breathing through his nose, Tim cracked his knuckles.

'Tim, you're getting lost. Come back to me, come look at me. It's Lou. We have a chance at happiness, come over here and talk to me,' Lou said.

He wasn't listening.

She was making headway with the crack in the door. If only her fingers weren't so torn. She opened the drawer under the bed again and took out Tim's small jewellery box. The gold cross was perfect for door-picking. Ah, that was better.

They were beyond noticing, these guys. She could do anything. 'Tim, please don't take a chance on what we have. I don't want to lose you. They'll comb through our lives after this: phone records, accounts,' she said. 'They'll know you stole from my mum and didn't help me. You'll be recalled, both of you.'

'Give me a minute, please, Lou. Don't you want to pay back your mother?'

She put her mouth at the crack, yelled this time: 'You already have plenty to pay back my mum. Why don't you pay her back now?'

'Shh,' he said.

She was rigid. There was boiling blood pumping inside of her.

‘If we play this right you’ll get away with this,’ Tim said.

‘Get away with what?’

‘You killed a man.’ He let the words hang for a moment. ‘Just give me one more second,’ he said. ‘We’ll back up your story. We all need this money. It’ll be good for all of us.’

They were performing their good-luck dance again.

‘Righty-oh,’ Tim said. ‘Here we go, here we go.’

It was his orgasm face again. Until…

The game appeared to be over. The pings did not sound happy. There were no bells. Tim was frozen, silent, orgasm face turning pale.

‘What just happened?’ Rob said. ‘What just happened what just happened what just happened?’

‘Shit,’ Tim said, banging the desk with his fist, standing. ‘Shit shit. Fuck fuck fucking fuck.’

Rob took his phone from Tim and looked at his balance – minus five hundred. He dropped the phone, took a mighty swing and smashed his fist into Tim’s face.

CHAPTER TWENTY-TWO

Rob was still kicking.

She should probably tell him to stop.

Poor Tim, foetal on the floor, hands covering his face. 'I have an idea,' he said. 'Get her phone. Lou, I need your thumb.'

'Fuck you,' Rob said, kicking him in the side again.

'Fuck you,' Lou said to herself.

'Listen to me,' said Tim. 'I'll go to the Big Bet site this time. I always win big there, every time. I won four hundred thousand once. I have an account. I can get you at least fifty K if you get Lou's phone for me. You and Stacey could move to the Maldives.'

Rob thought about it. He had little to lose, and had relinquished his decision-making to depressants, stimulants and Tim. 'Which phone is hers?'

Tim pointed to Lou's phone, which was on the desk.

As Rob walked towards her she prayed he wouldn't notice that the crack was wider.

'Thumb,' he said, holding up her iPhone.

Bummer, the crack was not wide enough to get another finger through and take hold of the handset. Next time, she thought, obeying the order.

She couldn't keep watching as Tim went through her phone. What a brutal fly-on-the-wall view of her beloved she was getting. She wondered what she might have spied of Alan's life: he and Frieda boat-shopping perhaps or fucking Frieda-style, both parties alive. Alan hated that. Lou crouched below the crack and picked away, one thin sliver at a time.

'Done.' Tim had finished typing.

'What have you done?' said Rob, who was slumped on the sofa, probably entering the hangover stage.

'I've sent a film of Lou's to the wife of her sugar daddy. It's quite complicated. They're millionaires, own hotels and hostels and you name it.'

Just when she thought she'd gotten away from all that.

'Hang on, hang on – sugar daddy?' Rob wanted all the details.

'For two years. He paid for her penthouse on the beach, eight thousand a month, jewellery.'

'She's a fuckin' prostitute?' Rob said.

'Who are you to judge?' Tim said.

She was okay with being called a prostitute. Fuck it, who cared? But Tim had just put her in the same category as the sexual assaulter, frotter and flasher.

'Stacey told me,' Rob said, slapping his thigh. 'She called it! Fuck me. Fuck me for a tenner, she's a whore, a fucking whore. Wait till I tell Trace.'

Lou picked at the door faster. This didn't look like it was going to end well. For one thing, Tim's email would never work. Formidable Frieda would rather pay a hitman than Lou. Although she'd do anything to keep her Toorak/Portsea reputation safe.

Ping.

'No way,' Tim said, standing. 'No fucking way. It's from Frieda Bainbridge: "We've been expecting this for some time," she says. "Please docusign the attached non-disclosure agreement. We have adjusted the standard fifty-thousand-pound (hundred-thousand-dollar) fee to the ten thousand pounds you have requested. Payment will be transferred immediately upon receipt of signature under the heading: Return of Rental Deposit. Frieda Bainbridge." What a bitch,' Tim said.

Right?! Lou said to herself.

Tim held up the phone for Lou to docusign. She could just about grab it from the bottom with her thumb and forefinger. The crack needed to be a tiny bit bigger next time. She lay on the bed and worked as quietly as she could. It sounded like the boys were finishing off what remained of Doug's last hurrah. Tim wasn't so worried about DNA anymore. They must be wasted. She wondered what their next step would be if Frieda failed to cough up. Would they go over to the flat, rob Becks? She could not let that happen. Not to beautiful Becks.

She heard the ping, and the squeals of delight from the two men in the room adjacent.

Frieda was a woman of her word. She had coughed up.

Rob had only just started doing a jig – 'Maldives here we come' – when Tim smiled at him and held up the screen of Lou's phone:

Her account balance: £46,700.

'How…' Rob was confused, 'but it was ten, five each, what … £46,700?'

'Told you, I win on this baby every time,' Tim said.

'Just bet half of it,' said Rob, in deep now. He checked that he was standing the right distance behind his new best friend forever. He began his nasal breathing. 'Just half, then no more.'

The cracking of knuckles turned to the sounds of the casino. Two seconds later, the men were screaming, laughing, banging each other's backs in the name of a hug, jumping up and down because they had won…

'£104,875,' Rob said, reading the screen balance again. '£104,875. I can hardly breathe.'

'Did that just happen, did that just happen?' Tim was pacing and punching the air because he was a winner, a winner, baby, yasss, that just happened.

'One more time,' Rob said. 'This could sort us for life.'

'You took the words right outta my mouth,' said Tim. 'I need a wee and a drink first.' They wandered out into the hall.

Lou's hands were bleeding from splinters and from the cut that happened so many major incidents ago, but, at last, the crack was wide enough. Next time they needed her thumb, she would get hold of her handset, pull it through to the safe side, and this would be over.

Her hands were shaking. If they lost the bet this time – all that money, that life-changing money – things would turn ugly. Things were probably going to turn ugly anyway. She rummaged through the other boxes under the bed for weapons and gathered a tie, a pair of scissors and a bottle of vodka, from which she took two large gulps. She remembered Tim's watch – could be useful round her knuckles – and added it to her weapons pile. She then opened the small jewellery box that she'd taken the gold cross from. It must have come with a chain. Perhaps it was hiding behind the foam. She jiggled it. There was something there.

She unpicked the foam from the jewellery box and looked inside. There was no chain, just a ring.

A sapphire ring, surrounded by diamonds; with an inscription under the rim: *Elvin and Eunice*. A love heart was the full stop.

Tim's mother's engagement ring; the one that was stolen by the burglar.

Lou slipped the ring on her finger and vomited in the urine-filled sink. Seventeen-year-old Tim *had* stolen the contents of the safe that night. He was the masked burglar, the parent murderer. He needed to be put in a sack with a bunch of snakes and chucked in a lake.

She needed to get ready for a fight.

First, a stronger barricade. She unplugged the mini fridge, slid it across the room and lifted it onto the bed.

'What was that?' Tim said.

He was not referring to the fridge. There was a tapping sound outside, another, a bang. Lou looked out the window. It was Sam and Tony, come to break Doug's legs.

'Fuck,' said Tim, who had obviously looked out the office window. 'How much does he owe them again – five grand, wasn't it?'

But Tim wasn't about to allow some petty five-grand drug debt ruin the best night he'd had in over a decade, a winning spree to match his intoxicating, as yet unbeaten, first. He would sort this, quick smart.

'Five thousand,' said Rob. 'He never stopped begging me for it.'

'Best to pay them, right?' said Tim.

'Yep,' said Rob.

What a team they were turning out to be.

Lou tried to get Sam and Tony's attention without making a sound – she waved, she mouthed 'Help'. It was no use. One of the brothers had been hit by a rock that ricocheted off Doug's window, poor thing. The other one was comforting him, his hand on his brother's shoulder. They were sitting on the railings next door. She wished they would turn around and see her. Instead, they began tapping away on their phones.

In the office adjacent, Doug's phone replied with beeps. Eventually, Tim answered it. 'Hi Sam,' he said. 'Doug's with me, he's been expecting you. He's going to pay that in right now. Yep, wait on the phone while he transfers it. You done it yet, Doug?' he said, busy on the phone making the transfer himself. 'He's sending it to Samuel Barr, yes? Okay, that's done. You got it? Excellent.' He hung up and looked at Doug. 'You can rest in peace now.'

Outside, Sam and Tony were pocketing their phones. They were standing up, shaking themselves off, smiling. They had their revenge, and their money. One of the brothers yawned, the other did too. It was time for them to head home to bed.

'Are they going?' Tim said.

'They're about to,' Rob said. He was obviously on lookout at the office window, getting the same view as Lou.

'Help!' Lou screamed. It was time to make a noise. She banged on the window. 'Help me!'

Rob and Tim yelled at her in tandem. She should shut the fuck up. If she didn't, bad things would happen.

She screamed at the top of her lungs. 'Help me!'

Tim ran over to the sleepover-room door, spitting through the crack with his 'Shhhhh.'

'They're not leaving,' Rob said.

'Lou, don't make a sound, please,' Tim said.

'They're heading to the door,' Rob said.

'Let me get rid of them,' Tim said. 'Please, Lou, don't make a sound, yeah. You're safest in there, you really are.'

Was she safest in there? She had thought so, until she found the ring.

'They're knocking,' said Rob.

'Excuse me!' A voice was coming from outside the office, maybe from upstairs. 'Excuse me?' It was Lunchbox. 'Get the door,' he yelled. 'Someone get the frigging door.'

Sam and Tony had stopped knocking and were now pounding.

'Where's the night worker?' Lunchbox yelled from upstairs. 'Night worker? Answer the door!'

Tim took a deep breath. 'Okay, Rob, get everything you can out of the locker and get ready in case.' He opened Raymond the Backpack, retrieved the keys and handed them to Rob. 'I'll send Lunchbox to bed, then get rid of those two, even if it takes another five grand. You all right with that?'

'Bargain if they fuck off,' Rob said, retrieving weapons from the locker. So far, he had two baseball bats, three knives and a sword. They made Lou's pile look a little sad.

'You'll be quiet, Lou?'

Lou was dizzy and very nauseous. 'I'll be quiet,' she said.

Sam and Tony were looking directly at her from outside

the front door. One of them threw a stone at the office window. They were smiling at her, giving her the thumbs-up. They were going to save her.

But she was in charge. Fuck, she was in charge. She should not let anyone enter a building with a corpse, four nutcases and an armoury, especially decent guys like Sam and Tony. She changed her mind. They should not come in. 'Don't,' she screamed. 'Sam, Tony, don't come in. Go home, please, it's not safe here.'

Rob was poised, sword in hand, at the office door. 'Tim's opening the door now,' he said to Lou in a loud whisper. 'He's telling them … Hang on, hang on, okay. Tim's told them how you're detoxing in there. They want to know you're okay. Tim wants you to yell out to them.'

'I'm okay!' Lou yelled. 'Sorry about that. I'm just detoxing!'

Rob put his ear back to the door. 'Can you yell it louder?'

'I'M OKAY,' Lou yelled. 'SORRY ABOUT THAT. I'M JUST DETOXING.'

'Tim's giving them another five grand,' Rob said.

There was a loud crash on the stairs. Lou jumped. 'What was that?'

'No. No, no. Lunchbox is back. He stumbled, he's okay,' Rob said. 'Shit, one of them is saying "Do I know you?" Shit, shit, they've both recognised him.' Rob scratched his head in discomfort. 'They're calling him a filthy paedo and a beast, they're saying how their ma was raped when she was little and that everything went wrong after that. They're saying they want to give him a doing. They're asking Tim if they can kick him a bit.'

'What's Tim saying?'

Rob didn't have time to answer because Lunchbox was screaming in agony. 'OOOOOWWWWW, not the face, not the face. Help. Owww, not the face! Help, someone help me.'

Rob covered his face with a hand. 'Should I stop them?'

It was a dilemma. They were both giving it a good think when Lunchbox finally stopped screaming.

Lou looked out the window. She watched Sam and Tony disappear round the corner, unsure if it made her feel better or worse.

When Tim came back into the office, he was stressed, breathless.

'Did they hurt him bad?' Rob asked.

'He'll be fine. Can you take him upstairs and put him to bed? Tell him and Chuggy not to come down till the cops make them. I'll disable the stairlift and go get frozen peas for his eye.'

'Back-right of the second bottom drawer,' Lou found herself saying. She had lined up her weapons on the windowsill. She had a decent barricade. But she was shaking like crazy.

'I'll just be two minutes,' Tim said. And this time, he *was* only two minutes, and was no longer stressed but excited. All distractions had been dealt with, crises averted. 'Any of that whisky left?' He found a bottle, had a swig, took out Lou's phone. 'I need your thumb again, please,' he said, holding it up to the crack, fingers clawing the handset on every side. She didn't even get close to grabbing it.

Tim readied himself for the last bet of the night. It was life-changing and a certainty. They were going to win. 'We are going to win,' he said, taking his seat without looking at her.

'We are going to win,' Rob said, moving into position.

CHAPTER TWENTY-THREE

It was getting harder to keep calm. Lou kept reminding herself that she was safer in the sleepover room, as long as they couldn't get in. She would stay focused, ready herself, pick away the splinters. She didn't know what time it was, maybe around 4.30am. It'd be light by six. Perhaps she could get Pastel – or someone else's – attention in the daylight. At the very least, Lunchbox and Chuggy might come down, despite strict orders to the contrary. If not, a worker would arrive for handover at nine.

Every few minutes she peeked through the crack in the door. It was unremarkable, watching two men gamble online, and Lou had to agree with her dad that spectators were idiots. He never watched footy with his pals. What a waste of time, he said. He played footy though, Saturdays four to six. He never watched someone fishing on the telly, either – he fished. Busy, busy, busy, every moment counted, life was short. As Lou watched Rob watch Tim watch the phone, she realised that her father's irritating opinions were seriously admirable. Stupidity was hard to watch. Rob thought he was doing something important. If someone dared to interrupt his focus right now, he would lose it, even if it was his beloved arsehole of a wife, Stacey. Rob didn't even have the important job of pressing the screen every now and again, like Tim did. Nevertheless he filled his role with angst, as if the manner of his spectating would have an effect on the outcome. He was careful not to move from his position, careful not to breathe noisily. He was as important to winning as Tim was. He may as well have been in an actual physical casino, watching his actual physical new best friend forever pressing an actual button.

Their faces made the same moves – from terror to dread to hope to ecstasy to anxiety – each emotion ephemeral. Round and round it went. *Come on, come on, yes, yes, yes … NO; what is happening, what is happening, NO, fuck YES. Did that just happen? NO, that did not just happen. YES.* Their mouths always told the same lie after a bet – one last time, just one more, just one last time – and until it was agreed the mood was grim. The casino had probably only been pinging for twenty minutes. It seemed like hours.

Hang on. They'd stopped. There was silence. No breathing. Then both men screamed and bounced from their frozen positions, about one foot in the air, Tim from his seat, Rob from standing. They roared and they bounced, both standing now, trying to be as tall as they possibly could. They held hands and bounced in a circle, they bounced their stomachs against each other. They could not breathe. Had that just happened? Did that just happen?

'Oh my god. Oh my god, give me the phone. We're not going again,' Rob said, keen to stop bouncing.

'No, I promised, we are not going again,' said Tim. 'Why would we, why the fuck would we?' He was practically singing.

'Give me the phone.' Rob held out his sweaty, shaky hand. It would take a while for him to get his breath back.

Tim handed Lou's phone over, pleased with himself. He knew when to stop after all.

The two men lay on their backs on the spewy carpet tiles. They huffed and puffed and giggled. Sometimes they needed to hold their stomachs. What just happened?

'What did just happen?' said Lou from her room next door.

'We just won eight hundred thousand pounds,' Rob said. The men laughed again, had to hold their stomachs again.

'Just give us two minutes more,' Tim said from his horizontal heaven, 'just two minutes to get the smiles off our faces, then we'll call.'

'You can keep my share of the money if you let me out,' Lou said.

'Well, thank you, very kind considering you have no share. We did not negotiate a share for Lou, did we, Tim? Or are you sharing your half again, two hundred each?'

'I'm happy to share,' Tim said.

Happy to share! 'You should clean up,' Lou said. 'Get rid of any evidence that you were here. I don't care about my share, whatever. And I'll say whatever you want me to say. You can trust me.'

'You're right,' Tim said, sitting up. 'It'll get light soon too. We need to put everything back the way it was when Rob walked in. How long ago was that – about ninety minutes/two hours ago? The last two hours did not happen,' he said, wiping surfaces, bottles, laptops, anything he could think of, with his sleeve or the bottom of his T-shirt. 'So imagine it's two hours ago,' he said, owning the room, 'when we didn't have eight hundred thousand pounds…'

'Eight hundred thousand pounds!' Rob and Tim had to bounce again.

'So it's two hours ago. Me, Lunchbox and Chuggy are asleep in bed, have been since Doug drugged us with hot chocolate at around midnight. Rob, who didn't feel like his drink, heard some commotion and walked in to find Doug and then vomited all over the place. Got that, Rob?'

'Not really.'

'When I go back up to bed, you dial 999 and say this: "I just heard some noise, came down, and found Doug dead and the new night worker locked in the sleepover room." Can you say that? Then you tell the police that me, Lunchbox, Chuggy are still asleep. You say, "Help, I need an ambulance and the police." Got it?'

'You need to put my money in my account first,' Rob said, picking up Lou's phone.

'Shit, of course. Before we do anything, I need to make the transfers, then I go to bed, then Rob calls 999. Has everyone got it? We all need to say exactly the same thing.' He went over it again, word for word. 'Got it, Lou?'

'You used my account for your betting?' she said.

Tim looked worried, rightly.

'And how much is my share again,' she found herself saying, 'out of eight hundred thousand pounds?' She was thinking about money more than she should. But eight hundred thousand pounds was currently in her account and she did not feel like handing it over to a double murderer and a sex offender. Even though it would all be null and void after the police arrived, surely? Maybe not. Probably. Fuck them. 'I want half,' she said. 'Four hundred thousand.'

'Fuck that,' Rob yelled.

'A third each,' Tim said.

'Fuck that,' Rob said.

'Deal,' Lou said.

Tim didn't seem annoyed. She should have asked for more.

'Good,' he said. 'Rob, that's 267,000 pounds each. A lot, otherwise it could be nothing. This is going to work out for everyone if we do it quick smart. And we get our stories straight.' He went over it again. 'Got it? Cool, we're nearly done here. Thumb please, Lou.'

Tim held up the phone, not noticing that the crack was more of a gorge.

It was time. She squatted, out of sight. She held up her left thumb and pressed it against the screen.

'It's not working,' Tim said.

'Lift it up a bit,' Lou said, still pressing the wrong thumb against the phone while getting in position. She was ferreting with her dad, crouched by the opening, waiting for the rabbit to come out.

Tim lifted the phone, not quite enough, not quite enough, nearly enough.

She flicked the handset from his grasp, grabbed it with her right hand and pulled it through. *Thank god.* She raced over to the window, as far away from him as she could get, and pressed her thumb – one last time – against the phone. It didn't work. She had a splinter on the tip of her right thumb. What was Becks's birthday? *011299?* No luck.

'Hey Lou, come on, don't be daft. This can work out for us both. Can you give me the phone please?' Tim said.

'Give him the phone,' Rob yelled. 'Give him the phone, you fucking whore.'

Tim waited a moment, then punched the door, weakening the top half, the crack getting wider, the fridge inching off the bed.

Lou pulled out the splinter in her thumb and sucked the blood as Tim continued to punch the door.

Rob, meanwhile, was freaking out. Everything was going wrong. He was supposed to be going home to Stacey. 'Stop smashing things,' he was saying. 'Please Tim, stop. You're screwing everything up. Lou, just give him the phone.' Rob was weeping and pulling his hair and stamping his feet. 'Please, Lou. Please, Tim!'

Tim stopped for a moment, tried a different tack. 'Please. This works out for all of us. Think about it. Don't fuck it up now.'

'I'll give you the money later,' she said. 'What's the hurry? Don't you trust me?'

'Give it to me or I'll smash the door down,' Tim said.

She was sick of listening to Tim. *021299,* she tried to type, but her thumb was too sticky and wet for the digits to register. She sucked her thumb again, dried it on her grotty top.

Tim was now smashing what was left of the door with a baseball bat.

'Tim, no, stop, you're fucking with the crime scene. The plan, your plan, Tim. The DNA. Stop!' Rob was frantic. He almost sounded like a nice guy; like he was on her team.

Tim was not listening to him though. Pieces of door were falling on Doug's body and onto her barricade. Soon there would be no door and he would jump right through. 'Give me the phone NOW.'

'I am gonna get you for this,' Rob said, heading out the door. 'You've ruined everything. Everything. I fucking hate you. I was never here. I was never fucking here.'

Lou's thumb was still bleeding too much to open her phone. The battery was running low too. *031299*, she tried. She sucked her thumb, tried to dry it. Out the window, she saw Rob jogging, then walking, down Nevis Place. She'd bet he was heading to Polly's.

Lou looked at her arsenal on the windowsill: not great.

A loud bang made her drop her phone and it bounced off her foot. Tim was obliterating the door. She scoured the floor for her phone but couldn't find it.

She leapt towards the bed, grabbed the pole that still was in Doug's head, and pulled as hard as she could. It took three yanks and at least one long groan for it to dislodge, which it did with a crack and a squelch. The curtain pole flew backward with her. Her back smashed into the sink and her head hit a cupboard. It was bleeding, ouch. The pole was bladeless (the end must have still been stuck inside Doug's skull) and it was bloody, but it was something. She held it firmly as she stood up, Tim hovering over her on the bed now.

'This can still work out,' he said, lowering himself onto the floor, bat in hand. 'Just give me the phone.'

She took a step backward, towards the window. Her phone was somewhere around there. Several more steps and she had reached the window. She spotted her phone behind the bin. She picked it up and held it behind her back with one hand, pole outstretched with the other, shaking.

He took a step closer to her.

'Can I just put Rob's share in his account?' he said. 'He and Stacey will both come after us, you can count on that.'

'I can do it later,' Lou said.

'I'd like to do it now,' Tim said.

'What would you do to get my phone from me?' she said. 'Would you punch me, would you headbutt me? Would you kill me?'

Tim shook his head, almost as if he was coming to. He put the baseball bat in the sink. He put his hands in the air and took one step towards her. 'You still think I'm evil,' he said, tearing up.

'I'll do you a deal,' Lou said.

'Okay.' Tim relaxed.

Lou rested the end of the curtain pole against his stomach. 'You can either have my phone, which means you have eight hundred thousand pounds. Or…' She looked at her hand, at her wedding finger. He looked at it too. 'You can have your mother's engagement ring.'

Tim lunged at her but she was ready. She pressed the pole into his stomach and pushed. He fell back and she pinned him to the floor. She grabbed the vodka bottle from the windowsill and smashed him over the head, expecting it to shatter instead of thudding against his skull with a low crack of shifting bone. She took the scissors from the sill, knelt on his chest, pressed the blade against his neck. She could smell sandalwood.

'That was a shit deal,' Lou said, standing on him, then on the bed and scrambling into the office, her phone in hand. As she reached the front door, her thumb worked, at last.

'999, what's your emergency?' said the operator.

'Help me, help me,' Lou yelled into the handset. 'I need help.'

She ran out of the door.

CHAPTER TWENTY-FOUR

'I'm calling from the hostel on Nevis Place.' Lou was talking and running. 'My name is Lou O'Dowd.'

She made it across the road and banged on Pastel's door.

'There's one dead already.'

She rang his bell.

'I was taken hostage for hours. I'm the night worker at SASOL, number seven, Nevis Place, do you know it?'

'Where are you?'

'I'm across the road.'

'Stay on the line, knock on a neighbour's door, can you do that?'

'I have.'

'Help's on the way.'

She rang the bell again and the hall light went on. She could hardly breathe. She could hear footsteps, someone coming down the stairs. Her hands were shaking. She looked across the road at number seven. The door was still shut. He might come out any second. He might run over with his bat and bludgeon her head to mush. She rang the bell again.

The hall light went off. Pastel was not going to let her in. She crouched behind a bush in the front garden and looked at the other houses in the street, all the same as number seven, grumpy old buildings with invisible residents and who-knows-what going on inside. The only person she'd kind-of met was Posh Pastel, and he was a prick who wouldn't even answer the door.

She would not knock on any more doors.

Perhaps Tim was dying in there, though. Could the bottle have killed him? She should go over and check.

The cat flap swung open. Bertie. He meowed and made his way onto her lap.

'You're right, Bertie, I'll stay here.' She patted Bertie and watched the door of number seven until the police arrived.

She could drink cups of tea with Police Constable Mike Kearney forever. She might learn to enjoy surfing for Mike Kearney. He had scooped her up, and before she knew it she was on a gurney, in an ambulance, getting a cuppa and some drugs that were making her love Mike Kearney. He was holding her hand and that was all she needed to know.

'Poor little thing, of course you're the goodie. Anyone would look innocent up against those room-mates,' he said.

Lou liked Mike so much. The paramedic had given her something, mind, something gooood. She squeezed Mike's hand. How joyful to hold the hand of a dull good guy and to finally have the moral high ground and to have gotten off with murder and eight hundred grand.

The paramedics checked her head (concussion) and her hand (butterfly stitches for now). She might need a scan and proper stitches.

The back of the ambulance was open and Lou could see the front door, a balcony view of seven Nevis Place.

Tim had not come out yet. He may have escaped. This was a delicate situation.

Another ambulance parked beside Lou's, for Doug – no, probably for Tim. There were four police cars so far. Two officers had gone round the back, three were at the front gate. Another two were cordoning off the street and telling passers-by to bugger off. Lou could see a group of onlookers beyond the cordon, all pointing their phones at the door of number seven because something big was happening, apparently.

'Must be big,' one of the onlookers said to another. 'Someone must be dead inside, or injured at least, considering the ambulances. Shall we do a TikTok?'

Lou looked at the line of identical windows in the terraced houses of Nevis Place and gasped when she realised they were all filled with faces. Faces everywhere, looking out. She didn't recognise one of them. When did these people get in there? Where were they last night? Had they ever been out?

Pastel was standing on his steps, holding his cat. A group of clubbers, bare feet, holding heels, had stopped at the cordon to take selfies as Tim opened the front door and took a step outside, with his hands in the air.

Thank god, she hadn't killed him.

He was on the ground a second later, a tear or two running down his cheek. He spotted Lou in the ambulance. 'Lou,' he yelled, the whole world filming now. 'I'm sorry. It's gambling, makes my head crazy. I love you.'

A lot of awwwing was going on in the growing crowd. This was practically *Love Actually*.

Maybe it was the gentle squeeze from the hand of Mike Kearney that gave her the courage, and exactly the right words. She said nothing.

She really had nothing to say.

A few people may have clapped as the police bundled Tim into the van.

'Holy shit, is that Timmy the Kid?' she heard someone say.

'No way,' said another.

'It is. Fuck, that's Timmy the Kid. TikTok, shit, shit, is this happening? Hello from Nevis Place, Edinburgh, where right behind me Timmy the Kid is only getting his arse fucking *arresterated*. Stay tuned, share, I'm on live at Nevis Place where Timmy the Kid has just been arrested. What are you arresting him for?' he yelled at the police officer. 'Hey, what's the charge?'

'We believe you, Timmy,' someone yelled. One of the barefoot women.

As the police-van doors closed, Lou shook her head, like the blonde soccer mum did at the bar that time. *How could she still be so stupid?*

The angel on stilts had arrived to see the show. A group of school children too, all in neat private uniforms, all using their phones.

The commotion was getting louder in Nevis Place. A helicopter was hovering overhead. Mike half shut the door to continue questioning her: 'Do you know where Rob went?'

'He didn't say, maybe his wife's place in Livingston. Her name's Stacey. Or to Polly's. The boss.'

'I know who Polly is.'

'Not sure where she lives though.'

'I know where Polly lives,' he said.

Kearney relayed the information on his radio thingy: 'Mackenzie'll be at Polly's. Don't forget the basement and her allotment. As for the situation here, far as we know there's one dead in the ground-floor office to the front, Douglas Simpson, initiator, hostage taker, defensive and effective stab, there are two baseball bats, one sword and several knives in the office area. There are two men, who do not appear to have been involved, on the first floor, although we have not heard from them at all and they're not answering their phones, or the door. Bit worried to be honest. One is elderly and frail, one has no legs.' Kearney realised he was being filmed by an onlooker. 'Oi, move away. Get them back,' he said.'Yep,' said Kearney over his radio. 'That's who we're talking about ... Aye. Can someone get in touch with their parole officers immediately? The two most hated men in the country. I said get the crowds back,' Mike yelled. 'Move the cordons, tell those people to stop filming. No photos. Get back, back.'

A man had jumped the cordon and his face was suddenly in Kearney's: 'Is this a hostel or what?'

'Get out, get back, damn it.' Kearney pushed the man away. 'Get these people back,' he yelled.

'Is it true there's a disabled man and an elderly gentleman still stuck in the house?' the man yelled, now on the right side of the cordon. 'Are they alive? Who are they? Are they okay?'

She might have been hallucinating, but it seemed that the crowd was thickening by the second, people arriving every which way, whispering to each other, posting their whispers online.

The TikTok guy, for example, with his very loud voice: 'I can confirm there's one dead already, I don't know who, may he or she rest in peace. There's an old man and a disabled man still in the building, and a serious violent sex offender is at large. It has not been confirmed whether the two very vulnerable older gentlemen trapped in the house are alive, or dead.'

A loud bang came from within the house, shuddering the crowd, then silencing it. Several cops moved to cover the doorway.

The TikTok guy whispered: 'Something's going on inside. I don't know if that was a – maybe a … a gun going off. This is Frances Grange, live from the ongoing hostage crisis in Edinburgh, where fears are growing for the safety of a disabled man and a frail elderly gentleman.'

Lou could hear the story being passed on: one of the poor old guys had no legs.

Another loud bang came from inside: either something falling or something smashing, it was hard to tell. People started moving back from the cordon, they didn't stop filming though.

Another crash, much louder this time.

'What was that?' said the TikTok guy. The doorway was surrounded by armed police now – the big guns, literally. 'The police are moving in, they're moving in…' he said.

'Everyone come down with your hands up,' Kearney said, his voice still quiet despite the megaphone. The helicopters were drowning him out too. 'If you don't come out on the count of three we're coming in. One…'

You couldn't hear a sound bar the helicopter. The armed

police officers at the entrance, all pointing guns, were still and silent.

'Two,' Kearney said, stopping to listen to the sounds inside the hall.

He was about to say three when the door creaked open.

The officers cocked their guns; the crowd inhaled, held it in. There was nothing to see at first, just part of a dark hallway, then all of it. Then elderly Lunchbox, dressed in his lift shoes and his untied floral silk kimono, holding Chuggy Chatroom like a baby in his tiny, shaky arms. His legs wobbled one last step under the weight. He was outside now, in the light, visible to everyone, no hat, no wig, no sun-glasses, just a black eye and an heroic grin. He had made it. His legs shook violently, his arms the same. Someone needed to help him soon. Someone needed to catch the man in his arms, the disabled man, who was also grinning, and holding his thumb up.

There was absolute silence…

…followed by earth-shattering cheers and applause.

CHAPTER TWENTY-FIVE

In a halfway house in Edinburgh, Lou decided that she did not like bad boys and that she should never judge a city by its cover.

'You're trending,' someone said.

Lou wasn't sure where she was or who had said this. Eventually she opened her eyes. She was in hospital. The voice was Big Neil's.

'Hashtag YesPleaseLouise,' he said. 'LusciousLou is also catching on, then there's the obvious one, LeggyLou.' He was giggling away as he scrolled through his phone. '"Hot night worker impales robber through a hole in the door." Why the fuck did you not tell me you're so interesting? I mean, how do you make a spear like that?' he said. 'Hahaha. "Onlookers have clapping remorse as hero recognised as vile predator." Ha ha, look at this,' Neil said. '"Timmy the Kid and His Killer Girlfriend!"'

'People know about me and Tim?'

'Everyone knows about it now, ya dickhead. The whole world saw him say "I love you", remember?'

Lou couldn't remember much at all. They must have given her some serious painkillers. She was hashtag WoozyLoozy.

'His fans were all over this within minutes. There's JusticeForTimmy and FreeTimothy, loads. None of them like you very much.'

She wished Neil would stop talking.

'BetOnTim – says you killed his parents and set him up.'

'I would have been twelve years old when his parents were murdered.'

'BetOnTim says you're lying about your age.'

Low blow. 'I was in Australia.'

'Were you though? There have been sightings in Malta. How many skeletons are in your closet? This is going to be hard for you. "Bombshell Aussie Takes on Five Dangerous Men". I bet that *Sixty Minutes* programme in Australia will want to do an exclusive with you. How exciting would that be?'

A bit.

'Actually, if they ask, do not do it. No offence, but I really don't think you'll come over well.'

'Can you stop saying shit?' she said.

Neil put his phone down. 'Okay, sorry. David was here but he had to go. Serious incident going down at the women's unit. Poor Neens. David said to say sorry and not to worry about anything, take as much sick leave as you need. He needs to make some changes, but not you, if you ever need to work again. By the way, Rob was caught in Polly's basement. David listened to all my recordings and said they're invaluable. He said don't expect to see Polly at work again. They're sending her off to Social Worker Island.'

'Where's Social Worker Island?'

'No-one knows. What are you going to do now? Do you think they'll let you keep the eight hundred thousand pounds?'

'No,' she said. 'I don't know.'

'I reckon they will: your money, your phone, your account. You could go anywhere, do anything. You could live on a yacht in the Med and make the staff do demeaning things.'

'Have you got my phone?' She sat up suddenly, in a panic.

'It's here,' Neil said, taking it from the small drawer. 'It's out of charge now. Do you have your charger?'

She only had her bum pack and its contents: Visa card, keys, all the things Doug had played with.

Neil was back on his phone, reading things to her again: 'Tim's sister's doing interviews online. Says she's spoken to Tim and he's sorry about what happened, that it was a relapse, gambling. She's decided it's in his best interests *not* to share the sale of Tavisdale with him. Oh shit.'

'How long have I been here?' Lou said. 'Do you know the time?' There wasn't even a clock on the wall.

Neil checked his phone. 'It's 14.45.'

She tried to get out of bed but there was something stuck in her arm. She ripped it out. 'Can you give me a lift?'

She put on her blood- and dust-covered clothes and ran through the shiny hospital corridors, turning back occasionally to make sure Big Neil was keeping up. He was, but it was killing him. They were both greatly relieved when they made it to the exit.

Neil's car was an enormous suburban number with two baby seats in the back. The huge vehicle did not surprise her, but the babies did. She wouldn't be dossing on his sofa.

Neil was the kind of careful and polite driver Lou wanted to punch in the face. She checked the well-lit clock on the dashboard. Five to three.

'Oh, honey,' Neil said, putting his hand on her shoulder.

She was crying. It was coming from the very bottom of her, erupting all the way up and out. There was nothing she could do to stop it. 'How do you do that job?' she said.

'You get used to it.'

'They're so scary.' Lou was convulsing, unable to talk. She wanted her mum and dad really badly. She hadn't eaten for hours and hours. She imagined lamingtons on a picnic blanket, and it made her sob harder.

Eventually she calmed herself. 'How do I look?' she said.

'It's impossible for you to look bad,' Neil said, parking the car.

She smiled.

'But today you have managed.' He had a brush and wipes in the glove compartment. He set to work.

'You must be a lovely dad,' she said as he wiped something sticky from her cheek.

'No, no, do not start up again,' he said. 'No crying. You're going to be okay. You'll need some counselling and medication, obviously, but you will be okay. Go to the doctor, yeah? And I am here for you, anytime. Can I please come with you?'

'No, it's fine,' she said.

He kissed her on the clean part of her cheek and watched her walk down towards The Caves.

There was no-one in the lane, or in the queue. She was late. She was a terrible cousin and friend.

'Sorry, she didn't leave you a ticket,' the gatekeeper said, checking the list.

'Please can I go in?' Lou said.

'Of course, if you pay,' said the gatekeeper.

Lou had forgotten how things worked. She could pay. The gatekeeper gave her a ticket and almost pushed her into the theatre.

The curtains were still closed, the lights were still on. She had made it on time.

She had made it on time!

Unlike the first time, the theatre was packed. Cam and

Giuseppe were in the front row. Some official-looking types were behind them. Cate Blanchett's people's people in London, maybe. There was a reverence in the space. Everyone was silent, actually hoping for *Plath! The Musical* to begin.

There was an aisle seat three rows from the back, thank god. She fell into it. The woman beside her sniffed, moved as far away from her as she could, which was not very. The seats were tiny. Surely Neil would have told her if she smelt. Although he did have two baby seats in the back. Urine probably smelt fine to him.

Urine. Oh my god, the police would see the tide mark in the sink. Maybe they'd film it and the footage would wind up on *Sixty Minutes* for the whole world to see.

The lights were too bright. Her head was pounding.

The person in front of her had put a puffer coat over the back of the seat. It was thick and soft. She wanted to bury her head in it. She stroked it. She wanted to live in it.

She was going to need to live somewhere, after all.

Cam was going to Tuscany, apparently. It looked beautiful there. She could hunt for mushrooms in the woods. She could dance at outside festas that celebrated polenta or pigs' knuckles. She could read serious novels under the shade of a cypress tree and buy fresh ricotta from her neighbour's kitchen. She'd have to learn the language, of course. She hated learning. She hated living in the country too. And ricotta.

Her mum had her room ready. 'And we'll get your ticket home,' she'd said when they spoke in the ambulance. They were in Brissie now, not out on some base. But Lou couldn't do that to them. Or to herself. She didn't want to live with her parents. She was twenty-three, for fuck's sake.

The puffer coat was like a duvet, so soft.

No, she wanted to live in a city where she was not expected to be successful, where no-one would judge her for staying indoors for days on end, or for crying suddenly in a supermarket. Neil said he knew somewhere like that, and that it wasn't too far away.

The lights faded and the curtains opened. A fifties housewife was stirring something on the cooker. More likely she was stirring nothing, as her large metal spoon banged against the saucepan like a drum: *boom boom, boom boom…*

Lou must not faint. She must not vomit. She must not rest her head on a stranger's puffer jacket nor close her eyes.

She could breathe, and breathe, and focus, and breathe.

She could see Becks, at the side of the stage. Could Becks see her?

Becks saw her! Her smile. Aww, little Becks. Right now, she looked just like Lou's dad. Lou's lips went all quivery – Becks, her best friend.

Lou put her hand on her heart, mouthed *I love you.*

Her cousin did the same.

Becks looked like a movie star, she'd say after. She'd say

she's so proud to know her, that she's amazing, that she had tingles. She'd say she loved the set and the sound-effects, the spoon and saucepan going *boom, boom, boom, boom* like that, so loud that it even seemed like it might be echoing. It was hypnotic, she'd say. It sounded even better with her head down, resting on the puffer jacket a little, just a little. Even better if she closed her eyes and focused and breathed in time with the beat of the spoon against the saucepan by the sad woman in vintage. *Boom*, Becks was so clever, she was a movie star. *Boom, boom, boom, boom. Boom, boom, boom, b…*

She woke to clapping.

ACKNOWLEDGEMENTS

Thanks to the supportive and brilliant team at Orenda – especially Karen Sullivan, West Camel, Anne Cater, Cole Sullivan, Max Okore, and Danielle Price.

Thanks to Martin Hughes and the team at Affirm Press in my other hometown, Melbourne.

Thanks to my literary agent, Philip Paterson at Marjacq Scripts, and to Luke Speed at Speed Literary and Talent Management.

To Yvonne at Soho for her hilarious stories and her JUICY suitcase.

A big thank-you to the lovely Luisa Gillies for the early read and excellent feedback.

To Sarah P for reading and for the funniest anecdotes ever.

To the brilliant Jane Montgomery Griffiths for the musical advice.

To Serge, for being a brilliant, generous and fun writing partner.

Lastly, thank you to Edinburgh, for my first job in Scotland. And to Glasgow, for saving me from it.